Bart Stirling's Road to Success; Or, the Young Express Agent

Allen Chapman

ESPRIOS DIGITAL PUBLISHING

A PIECE OF ROPE WAS LOOPED DEFTLY ABOUT BART'S ARMS.
Bart Stirling's Road to Success

BART STIRLING'S ROAD TO SUCCESS

Or

The Young Express Agent

BY

ALLEN CHAPMAN

AUTHOR OF "THE HEROES OF THE SCHOOL," "NED WILDING'S DISAPPEARANCE," "FRANK ROSCOE'S SECRET," "FENN MASTERSON'S DISCOVERY," "BART KEENE'S HUNTING DAYS," ETC., ETC.

NEW YORK

CUPPLES & LEON COMPANY

1908

THE BOYS' POCKET LIBRARY

BY ALLEN CHAPMAN

Cloth. Illustrated. Price per volume, 35 cents, postpaid.

THE HEROES OF THE SCHOOL
NED WILDING'S DISAPPEARANCE
FRANK ROSCOE'S SECRET
FENN MASTERSON'S DISCOVERY
BART KEENE'S HUNTING DAYS
BART STIRLING'S ROAD TO SUCCESS
WORKING HARD TO WIN
BOUND TO SUCCEED
THE YOUNG STOREKEEPER
NED BORDEN'S FIND

CUPPLES & LEON CO, Publishers, New York

CONTENTS

CHAPTER I   THE THIRD OF JULY

CHAPTER II   "WAKING THE NATIVES"

CHAPTER III   COUNTING THE COST

CHAPTER IV   BLIND FOR LIFE

CHAPTER V   READY FOR BUSINESS

CHAPTER VI   GETTING "SATISFACTION"

CHAPTER VII   WAITING FOR TROUBLE

CHAPTER VIII THE YOUNG EXPRESS AGENT

CHAPTER IX   COLONEL JEPTHA HARRINGTON

CHAPTER X   QUEER COMRADES

CHAPTER XI   "FORGET IT!"

CHAPTER XII   THE MYSTERIOUS MR. BAKER

CHAPTER XIII "HIGHER STILL!"

CHAPTER XIV   MRS. HARRINGTON'S TRUNK

CHAPTER XV   AN EARLY "CALL"

CHAPTER XVI   AT FAULT

CHAPTER XVII A FAINT CLEW

CHAPTER XVIII A DUMB FRIEND

CHAPTER XIX   FOOLING THE ENEMY

CHAPTER XX   BART ON THE ROAD

CHAPTER XXI   A LIMB OF THE LAW

CHAPTER XXII BART STIRLING, AUCTIONEER

CHAPTER XXIII "GOING, GOING, GONE!"

CHAPTER XXIV MR. BAKER'S BID

CHAPTER XXV   A NIGHT MESSAGE

CHAPTER XXVI   ON THE MIDNIGHT EXPRESS

CHAPTER XXVII   LATE VISITORS

CHAPTER XXVIII THIRTY SECONDS OF TWELVE

CHAPTER XXIX   BROUGHT TO TIME

CHAPTER XXX   "STILL HIGHER!"

CHAPTER I

THE THIRD OF JULY

"You can't go in that room."

"Why can't I?"

"Because that's the orders; and you can't smoke in this room."

Bart Stirling spoke in a definite, manly fashion.

Lemuel Wacker dropped his hand from the door knob on which it rested, and put his pipe in his pocket, but his shoulders hunched up and his unpleasant face began to scowl.

"Ho!" he snorted derisively, "official of the company, eh? Running things, eh?"

"I am—for the time being," retorted Bart, cheerfully.

"Well," said Wacker, with an ugly sidelong look, "I don't take insolence from anyone with the big head. I reckon ten year's service with the B. & M. entitles a man to know his rights."

"Very active service just now, Mr. Wacker?" insinuated Bart pleasantly.

Lem Wacker flushed and winced, for the pointed question struck home.

"I don't want no mistering!" he growled. "Lem's good enough for me. And I don't take no call-down from any stuck-up kid, I want you to understand that."

"You'd better get to the crossing if you're making any pretense of real work," suggested Bart just then.

As he spoke Bart pointed through the open window across the tracks to the switch shanty at the side of the street crossing.

A train was coming. Mr. Lemuel Wacker was "subbing" as extra for the superannuated old cripple whose sole duty was to wave a flag as trains went by. To this duty Wacker sprang with alacrity.

Bart dismissed the man from his mind, and, whistling a cheery tune, bent over the book in which he had been writing for the past twenty minutes.

This was the register of the local express office of the B. & M., and at present, as Bart had said, he was "running it."

The express shed was a one-story, substantial frame building having two rooms. It stood in the center of a network of tracks close to the freight depot and switch tower, and a platform ran its length front and rear.

Framed by the window an active railroad panorama spread out, and beyond that view the quaint town of Pleasantville.

Bart had spent all his young life here. He knew every nook and corner of the place, and nearly every man, woman and child in the village.

Pleasantville did not belie its name to Bart's way of thinking. He voted its people, its surroundings, and life in general there, as pleasant as could well be.

Here he was born, and he had found nothing to complain of, although he was what might be called a poor boy.

There were his mother, his two sisters and two small brothers at home, and sometimes it took a good deal to go around, but Bart's father had a steady job, and Bart himself was an agreeable, willing boy, just at the threshold of doing something to earn a living and wide-awake for the earliest opportunity.

Mr. Stirling had been express agent for the B. & M. for eight years, and was counted a reliable, efficient employee of the company.

For some months, however, his health had not been of the best, and Bart had been glad when he was impressed into service to relieve his father when laid up with his occasional foe, the rheumatism, or to watch the office at mealtimes.

Bart was on duty in this regard at the present time. It was about five in the afternoon, but it was also the third of July, and that date, like the twenty-fourth of December, was the busiest in the calendar for the little express office.

Bart Stirling's Road to Success

All the afternoon Bart had worked at the desk or helped in getting out packages and boxes for delivery.

A little handcart was among the office equipment, and very often Bart did light delivering. On this especial day, however, in addition to the regular freight, Fourth of July and general picnic and celebration goods more than trebled the usual volume, and they had hired a local teamster to assist them.

With the 4:20 train came a new consignment. The back room was now nearly full of cases of fruit, a grand boxed-up display of fireworks for Colonel Harrington, the village magnate, another for a local club, some minor boxes for private family use, and extra orders from the city for the village storekeepers.

It was an unusual and highly inflammable heap, and when tired Mr. Sterling went home to snatch a bite of something to eat, and lazy Lem Wacker came strolling into the place, pipe in full blast, Bart had not hesitated to exercise his brief authority. A spark among that tinder pile would mean sure and swift destruction. Besides, light-fingered Lem Wacker was not to be trusted where things lay around loose.

So Bart had squelched him promptly and properly. The man for whom "Lem" was good enough, was in his opinion pretty nearly good for nothing.

Bart made the last entry in the register with a satisfied smile and strolled to the door stretching himself.

"Everything in apple-pie order so far as the books go," he observed. "I expect it will be big hustle and bustle for an hour or two in the morning, though."

Lem Wacker came slouching along. It was six o'clock, the quitting hour. Lem was always on time on such occasions. The whistle from the shops had ceased echoing, and, his dinner pail on his arm and filling his inevitable pipe, he paused for a moment.

"Going to shut up shop?" he inquired with affected carelessness.

"I am going home, if that's what you mean," replied Bart—"as soon as my father comes."

"Not feeling very well lately, eh?" continued Lem, his eyes roving in a covetous way over the cozy office and the comfortable railroad armchair Mr. Stirling used. "No wonder, he takes it too hard."

"Does he?" retorted Bart.

"You bet he does. Wish I had his job. I'd make people wait to suit my ideas. How's the company to know or care if you break your neck to accommodate people? Too honest, too."

"A man can't be too honest," asserted Bart.

"Can't he? Say, I'm an old railroader, I am, and I know the ropes. Why, when I was running the express office at Corydon, we sampled everything that came in. Crate of bananas—we had many a lunch, apples, cigars, once in a while a live chicken, and always a couple of turkeys at holiday time."

"And who paid for them?" inquired Bart bluntly.

"We didn't, and no questions asked."

"I am afraid your ideas will not make much impression on my father, if that is what you are getting at," observed Bart, turning unceremoniously from Wacker.

"Humph! you fellows ought to run a backwoods post office," disgustedly grunted the latter, as he made off.

Bart had only to wait ten minutes when his father appeared. Except for a slight limp and some pallor in his face, Mr. Stirling seemed in his prime. He had kindly eyes and was always pleasant and smiling, even when in pain.

"Well! well!" he cried briskly, with a gratified glance at his son after looking over the register, "all the real hard work is done, the work that always worries me, with my poor eyesight. Come up to the paymaster, young man! There's an advance till salary day, and well you've earned it."

Mr. Stirling took some money from his pocket. There was a silver dollar and some loose change. Bart looked pleased, then quite grave, and he put his hand resolutely behind him.

"I can't take it, father," he said. "You have a hard enough time, and I ought to pay you for the experience I'm getting here instead of being paid."

"Young man," spoke Mr. Stirling with affected sternness, but a twinkling in his eye, "you take your half-pay, make tracks, enjoy yourself, and don't worry about a trifle of a dollar or two. If you happen to drop around this way about nine o'clock, I'll be glad of your company home."

He slipped the money into Bart's pocket and playfully pushed him through the doorway. Bart's heart was pretty full. He was alive with tenderness and love for this loyal, patient parent who had not been over kindly handled by the world in a money way.

Then a dozen loud explosions over on the hill, followed by boyish shouts of enthusiasm, made Bart remember that he was a boy, with all a boy's lively interest in the Fourth of July foremost in his thoughts, and he bounded down the tracks like a whirlwind.

CHAPTER II

"WAKING THE NATIVES!"

Turning the corner of the in-freight house Bart came to a quick halt.

He had nearly run down a man who sat between the rails tying his shoe.

The minute Bart set his eyes on the fellow he remembered having seen him twice before—both times in this vicinity, both times looking wretched, dejected and frightened.

The man started up, frightened now. He was about forty years old, very shabby and threadbare in his attire, his thin pale face nearly covered with a thick shock of hair and full black beard.

"Hello!" challenged Bart promptly.

"Oh, it's you, young Stirling," muttered the man, the haunted expression in his eyes giving way to one of relief.

"Found a job yet?" asked Bart.

"I—haven't exactly been looking for work," responded the man, in an embarrassed way.

"I should think you would," suggested Bart.

"See here," spoke the man, livening up suddenly. "I'll talk with you, because you're the only friend I've found hereabouts. I'm in trouble, and you can call it hiding if you like. I'm grateful to you for the help you gave me the other night, for I was pretty nigh starved. But I don't think you'd better notice me much, for I'm no good to anybody, and I hope you won't call attention to my hanging around here."

"Why should I?" inquired Bart, getting interested. "I want to help you, not harm you. I feel sorry for you, and I'd like to know a little more."

A tear coursed down the man's forlorn face and he shook his head dejectedly.

"You can't sleep forever in empty freight cars, picking up scraps to live on, you know," said Bart.

"I'll live there till I find what I came to Pleasantville to find!" cried the man in a sudden passion. Then his emotion died down suddenly and he fell to trembling all over, and cast hasty looks around as if frightened at his own words.

"Don't mind me," he choked up, starting suddenly away. "I'm crazy, I guess! I know I'm about as miserable an object as there is in the world."

Bart ran after him, drawing a quarter from his pocket. He detained the man by seizing his arm.

"See here," he said, "you take that, and any time you're hungry just go up to the house and tell my mother, will you?"

"Bless her—and you, too!" murmured the man, with a hoarse catch in his throat. "I'll take the money, for I need it desperately bad, but don't you fret—it will come back. Yes! it will come back, double, the day I catch the man who squeezed all the comfort out of my life!"

He dashed away with a strange cry. Bart, half decided that he was demented, watched him disappear in the direction of a cheap eating house just beyond the tracks, and started homewards more or less sobered and thoughtful over the peculiar incident.

It was nearly eight o'clock when Bart got through with his supper, did his house chores, mended a broken toy pistol for one junior brother, made up a list of purchases of torpedoes, baby-crackers and punk for the other, and helped his sisters in various ways.

Bart was soon in the midst of the fray. Every live boy in Pleasantville was in evidence about the village pleasure grounds, the common and the hill. Group after group greeted Bart with excited exclamations. He was a general favorite with the small boys, always ready to assist or advise them, and an acknowledged leader with those of his own age.

He soon found himself quite active in devising and assisting various minor displays of squibs, rockets and colored lights. Then he got mixed up in a general rush for the sheer top of the hill amid the excited announcement that something unusual was going on there.

The crowd was met by a current of juvenile humanity.

"Run!" shouted an excited voice, "she's going off."

"No, she ain't," pronounced another scoffingly—"ain't lighted yet—no one's got the nerve to do it."

Bart recognized the last speaker as Dale Wacker, a nephew of Lem. He had noticed a little earlier his big brother, Ira, a loutish, overgrown fellow who had gone around with his hands in his pockets sneering at the innocent fun the smaller boys were indulging in, and bragging about his own especial Fourth of July supply of fireworks which were to come from some mysterious source not clearly defined. The Wacker brothers belonged to a crowd Bart did not train with usually, but as Dale espied him and seized his arm energetically, Bart did not draw away, respecting the occasion and its courtesies.

"You're the very fellow!" declared Dale.

"You bet he is!" cried two others, crowding up and slapping Bart on the back. "He won't crawfish. Give him the punk, Dale."

The person addressed extended a lighted piece of punk.

"Yes, take it, Stirling," he said. "Show him, boys."

"Yes, you'll have to show me," suggested Bart significantly. "What's the mystery, anyhow?"

"No mystery at all," answered Dale, "only a surprise. See it—well, it's loaded."

"Clean to the muzzle!" bubbled over an excited urchin.

They were all pointing to the top of the hill. Bart understood, for clearly outlined against the light of the rising moon stood the grim old sentinel that had done duty as a patriotic reminder of the Civil War for many a year.

"Old Hurricane" the relic cannon had been dubbed when what was left of Company C, Second Infantry, came marching back home in the sixties.

There was not a boy in town who had not straddled the black ungainly relic, or tried to lift the heavy cannon balls that symmetrically surrounded its base support.

Two years before, Colonel Harrington had erected at his own expense a lofty flagpole at the side of the cannon and donated an elegant flag. Every Washington's Birthday and Fourth of July since, this site had been the center of all public patriotic festivities, and the headquarters for celebrating for juvenile Pleasantville.

Bart was a little startled as he comprehended what was in the wind. He thrilled a trifle; his eyes sparkled brightly.

"It's all right, Stirling," assured Dale Wacker. "We cleaned out the barrel and we've rammed home a good solid charge, with a long fuse ready to light. Guess it will stir up the sleepy old town for once, hey?"

Bart was in for any harmless sport, yet he fumbled the lighted piece of punk undecidedly.

"I don't know about this, fellows"—he began.

"Oh! don't spoil the fun, Stirling," pleaded little Ned Sawyer, a rare favorite with Bart. "We asked one-legged Dacy on the quiet. He was in the war, and he says the gun can't burst, or anything."

The crowd kept pushing Bart forward in eager excitement.

"Why don't you light it yourself?" inquired Bart of Dale.

"I've sprained my foot—limping now," explained young Wacker. "She may kick, you see, and soon as you light her you want to scoot."

"Go ahead, Bart! touch her off," implored little Sawyer, quivering with excitement.

"Whoop! hurrah!" yelled a frantic chorus as Bart took a voluntary step up the hill.

That decided him—patriotism was in the air and he was fully infected. One or two of the larger boys advanced with him, but halted at a safe distance, while the younger ones danced about and stuck their fingers in their ears, screaming.

Bart got to the side of the cannon. It was silhouetted in the landscape on a slight slant towards the stately mansion and grounds of Colonel Harrington, in full view at all times of the magnate who had improved its surroundings.

Bart made out a long fuse trailing three feet or more over the side of the old fieldpiece. He blew the punk to a bright glow.

"Ready!" he called back merrily over his shoulder.

The hillside vibrated with the flutter of expectant juvenile humanity and a vast babel of half-suppressed excited voices.

Bart applied the punk, there was a fizz, a sharp hiss, a writhing worm of quick flame, and then came a fearful report that split the air like the crack of doom.

CHAPTER III

COUNTING THE COST

Bart had quickly moved to one side of the cannon after lighting the fuse, and was about twenty feet away when the explosion came.

The alarming echoes, the shock, flare and smoke combined to give him a terrific sensation.

The crowd that had retreated down the hill in delightful trepidation now came trooping back filled with a bolder excitement.

They had indeed "waked the natives," for gazing downhill against the lights of the street and stores at its base they could see people rushing outdoors in palpable agitation.

Some were staring up the hill in wonder and terror, others were starting for its summit, among them two village officials, as demonstrated by the silver stars they wore.

"They heard it—it woke 'em up, right enough!" shrieked little Sawyer in a frenzy of happiness.

"Look yonder!" piped a second breathless voice. "Say, I thought I heard something strike."

Dale Wacker came upon the scene—not limping, but chuckling and winking to the cronies at his back.

"Pretty good aim, eh, fellows?" he gloated. "Stirling, you're a capital gunner."

All eyes were now turned in a new direction—in that whither the muzzle of the cannon was pointed.

The grounds of the Harrington mansion were the scene of a vivid commotion. The porch lights had been abruptly turned on, and they flooded the lawn in front with radiance.

Bart gasped, thrilled, and experienced a strange qualm of dismay. He discerned in a flash that something heretofore always prominently present on the Harrington landscape was not now in evidence.

The wealthy colonel was given to "grandstand plays," and one of them had been the placing of a bronze pedestal and statue at the side of the driveway.

It bore the inscription "1812," and according to the colonel, portrayed a military man life-size, epaulettes, sword, uniform and all—his maternal grandfather as he had appeared in the battle scene where he had lost a limb.

Now, in effigy, the valiant warrior was prostrate. The colonel's servants were rushing to the spot where the statue had tumbled over on the velvety sward.

"See here!"—cried Bart stormingly, turning on Dale Wacker.

"Loaded," significantly observed the latter with a diabolical grin.

A rush of keen realization made Bart shiver. He recognized what the foolhardy escapade might have cost had that whirling cannon ball met a human, instead of an inanimate, target.

As it was, he easily calculated the indignation and resentment of the haughty village magnate who was given to outbursts of wrath which carried all before him.

"You've spoiled my Fourth," began Bart in a tumult. "I'll spoil your—"

"Cut for it, fellows! they're coming for us!"

"They" were the village officers. Bart had made a jump towards Dale Wacker, but the latter had faded into the vortex of pell-mell fugitives rushing away downhill to hiding.

Bart put after them, trying to single out the author of the scurvy joke that he knew had serious trouble at the end of it.

"Hold on!" gasped a breathless voice.

"Don't stop me!" shouted Bart, trying to tear loose from a frantic grip. "Oh, it's you—what do you want?"

He halted to survey the person who detained him—the man who haunted the freight tracks—to whom he had given money earlier in the evening.

"Come, quick!" the man panted. "Express shed—where your father is—trouble. Don't wait—not a minute."

"See here," challenged Bart, instantly startled into a new tremor of anxiety, "what do you mean?"

But the forlorn roustabout could not be coherent. He continued to gasp and splutter out excited adjectives, fragmentary sentences.

"Plot—get you into trouble—father—I heard 'em."

Then as his glance fell upon the people coming up the hill, the officers in their lead, his eyes bulged with terror, he grasped Bart's arm, let out an unearthly yell of fear, and by sheer force carried Bart pell-mell down the other side of the hill with him.

"See here," panted Bart, as, still running, they were headed in the direction of the railroad, "my business is here. Don't you hurry me off in this fashion unless there's something to it."

"Told you—express shed—robbers!"

"Robbers? You mean some one is stealing something there?"

"Yes!" gulped Bart's companion.

"Who is it?"

"Don't know."

"Why didn't you stop them?"

"I don't dare do anything," the man wailed. "I'm a poor, miserable object, but I'm your friend. I heard two fellows whispering on the tracks near the express shed. Said they were going to steal some fireworks. I ran to the shed to warn your father. He was asleep in his chair. They might see me—didn't dare do anything."

Bart now believed there might be some basis to the man's statements. He plunged forward alone, not conscious that he was outdistancing his late companion.

Reaching the tracks, Bart ran down a line of freights. The express shed was in view at last. It was lighted up as usual, the door stood open, and nothing suggested anything out of the ordinary.

Bart Stirling's Road to Success

"The fellow's cracked," reflected Bart. "Everything looks straight here—no, it doesn't!" He checked himself abruptly. "Here! what are you at?"

Sharp and clear Bart sang out. Approaching the express shed from the side, his glance shifted to the rear.

The little structure had one window there, lightly barred with metal strips. Two men stood on the platform beneath it. One of them had just pried a strip loose with some long implement he held in his hand. The other had just pushed up the sash by reaching through the convenient aperture thus made.

Bart bounded to the platform with a nimble spring. As his feet clamped down warningly on the boardway, the man who had pushed up the window turned sharply.

"It's young Stirling!" Bart heard him mutter. "Drop it, and run."

The speaker sprang to the ground and disappeared around the corner of the shed with the words.

His companion, who had been stooping on one knee in his prying operations, essayed to join him, slipped, tilted over, and before he could recover himself Bart was upon him.

"What are you about here?" demanded the latter.

The prisoner was of man-like build and proportions. He did not speak, and tried to keep his features hidden from the rays of the near switch light.

"Lemme go!" he mouthed, with purposely subdued intonation.

"Not till I know who you are—not till I find out what you're up to," declared Bart. "Turn around here. I'll stick closer than a brother till I see that face of yours!"

He swung his captive towards the light, but a broad-peaked cap and the partial disguise of a crudely blackened face defeated his purpose.

Bart was about to shout to his father in front, or to his roustabout friend, whom he expected must be somewhere near by this time, when his captive gave a jerk, tore one arm free, and whirled the other aloft.

His hand clenched the implement he had used to pry away the bars, and Bart now saw what it was.

The object the mysterious robber was utilizing for burglarious purposes, was the signal flag used at the switch shanty where Lem Wacker had been doing substitute duty that day.

It consisted of a three foot iron rod, sharpened at the end. At the blunt end the strip of red flag was wound, near the sharp end the conventional track torpedo was held in place by its tin strap.

"Lemme go"; again growled the man.

"Never!" declared Bart.

The man's left arm was free, and he swung the iron rod aloft. Bart saw it descending, aimed straight for his head. If he held on to the man he could scarcely evade it.

He let go his grip, ducked, made a pass to grasp the burglar's ankle, but missed it.

An explosion, a sharp flare, a keen shock filled the air, and before Bart could grip the man afresh he had sprung from the platform and vanished.

At the same instant the flag rod clattered to the boards, and a second later, rubbing his face free from sudden pricking grains of powder, Bart saw what had happened.

The blow intended for him had landed upon one of the iron bars of the window with a force that exploded the track torpedo.

It had flared out one broad spiteful breath, sending a shower of sparks among the big mass of fireworks in the storage room, and amid a thousand hissing, snapping explosions the express shed was in flames.

CHAPTER IV

BLIND FOR LIFE

Bart's first thought was of his father. He instantly leaped from the platform.

As he did so there was a violent explosion in the storage room, the sashes were blown from place outright, and Bart dodged to escape a shower of glass.

He was fairly appalled at the suddenness with which the flames enveloped the interior, for they shot up in every direction, and the partition dividing the shed appeared blown from place.

Rockets were fizzing, giant crackers exploding by the pack, and colored chemicals sending out a varied glow.

Bart dashed for the front—a muffled cry caused him to hurry his speed. His father had uttered the cry.

Dazed by the light, his eyes filled with smarting particles of burned powder, Bart suddenly came in violent contact with a human form just as he turned the corner of the shed.

Both nearly upset in the collision. At first Bart fancied it might be one of the burglars, but peering closer he recognized the friendly roustabout.

"Told you so!" gasped the latter in a desperate fluster. "Fire—I'll help you."

"Yes, quick! run," breathed Bart, rushing ahead, "My father's in that burning building!"

Bart was thrilled. The main room of the express shed was one bright blur of brilliancy and colored smoke.

It rolled and whirled, obliterating all outlines within the room.

"Father! father!" shouted Bart, dashing recklessly in at the open doorway.

He could not make out a single object in that chaos, but he knew the location of every familiar article in the place, and made for the chair in which his father usually sat.

"Father!" he screamed, as his hands touched the arms of the chair and found it empty.

The sulphurous flames nearly choked him, the heat from the crackling wooden partition singed his hair, but he could only grope about blindly.

"Here he is," sounded a suffocating voice.

"Where, oh! where?" panted Bart.

He threw out his arms wildly, groping to locate the speaker, whom he knew to be the roustabout. "Where is he—where is he?"

He had come in contact with the roustabout now, who with all his timidity was proving himself a hero in the present instance.

"Lying on the floor—stumbled over him—I'm on fire, too!"

Bart's feet touched a prostrate form. It was moved along as Bart stooped and got hold of the shoulders.

The roustabout was helping him. They dragged together, stumbling to the doorway on the very verge of fatal danger, and reeled across the platform.

The roustabout jumped to the ground. Once there he gently but in a masterly way drew the inanimate form of Mr. Stirling from the platform, and carried him over to a pile of ties outside of the glow and scorch of the burning express shed.

Bart anxiously scanned his father's face. It was black and blistered but he was breathing naturally.

"Overcome with the smoke—or tumbled and was stunned," declared the roustabout.

Excited approaching shouts caused the speaker to glare down the tracks. Half a dozen people were hurrying to the scene of the fire. The roustabout with a nervous gasp vanished in the darkness.

Bart was hovering over his father in a solicitous way as a night watchman and a freight crew appeared on the scene. There was a volley of excited questions and quick responses.

No means of extinguishing the flames were at hand. The newcomers suggested getting the insensible Mr. Stirling over to the street beyond the tracks a few hundred yards distant, where there was a drug store.

Bart ran for the hand truck on the platform, saw two of the men start off with his father on it, and hurried back to the burning express shed.

He had hoped to save something, but one effort drove him back, realizing the foolhardiness of repeating the experiment. The building and its contents were doomed.

The crowd began to gather and grew with the moments. A road official appeared on the scene. Bart made a brief, hurried explanation and ran over to the drug store.

To his surprise his father was not there. Bart approached the druggist to ask an anxious question when the companion of the latter, a professional-looking man, spoke up.

"You are young Stirling, are you not?" he interrogated.

"Yes, sir," nodded Bart.

"Don't get frightened or worried, but I am Doctor Davis. We thought it best to send your father to the hospital."

"To the hospital!" echoed Bart turning pale. "Then he is badly injured—"

"Not at all," dissented the physician reassuringly. "He was probably overcome by the smoke or fell and was stunned, but that injury was trifling. It is his eyes we are troubled about."

"Tell me the worst!" pleaded Bart in a choked tone, but trying to prepare himself for the shock.

"Why, one eye is pretty bad," said the doctor, "and the other got the full force of some powder explosion. They have good people up at the hospital, though, and they will soon get him to rights."

"I must tell my mother at once," murmured Bart.

He left the place with a heart as heavy as lead. It seemed as if one furious Fourth of July powder blast had disrupted the very foundations of all the family hopes and happiness, leaving a blackened wreck where there had been unity, comfort and peace.

If his father was disabled seriously, their prospects became a very grave problem. Bart, too, was worried about the loss to the express company. The books were probably out on the desk when the fire commenced, the safe was open, and the loss in money and records meant considerable.

Bart felt that he was undertaking the hardest task of his life when he reached home and broke the news to his mother—it was like disturbing the peace of some earthly Eden.

Mrs. Stirling went at once to the hospital with her eldest daughter, Bertha. Bart, very anxious and miserable, got the younger boys to bed and tried to cheer up his little sister Alice, who was in a transport of grief and suspense.

The strain was relieved when Bertha Stirling came home about eleven o'clock.

She was in tears, but subdued any active exhibition of emotion until Alice, on the assurance that her father was resting comfortably at the hospital, was induced to retire.

Then she broke down utterly, and Bart had a hard time keeping her from being hysterical.

She said that her mother intended staying all night at the side of her suffering husband and had tried to send some reassuring word to her son.

"You must tell me the worst, you know, Bertha," said Bart. "What do they say at the hospital? Is father in serious danger? Will he die?"

"No," answered the sobbing girl, "he will not die, but oh! Bart—the doctor says he may be blind for life!"

CHAPTER V

READY FOR BUSINESS

Bart Stirling stood ruefully regarding the ruins of the burned express shed. It was the Fourth of July, and early as it was, the air was resonant with the usual echoes of Independance Day.

Bart, however, was little in harmony with the jollity and excitement of the occasion. He had spent a sleepless night, tossing and rolling in bed until daybreak, when his mother returned from the hospital.

Mr. Stirling was resting easily, she reported, in very little pain or discomfort, but his career of usefulness and work was over—the doctors expressed an opinion that he would never regain his eyesight.

Mrs. Stirling was pale and sorrowed. She had grown older in a single night, but the calm resignation in her gentle face assured Bart that they would be of one mind in taking up their new burdens of life in a practical, philosophical way.

"Poor father!" he murmured brokenly. Then he added: "Mother, I want you to go in and get some rest, and try not to take this too hard. I will attend to everything there is to do about the express office."

"I don't see what there can be to do," she responded in surprise. "Everything is burned up, your father will never be able to resume his position. We are through with all that, I fancy."

"There is considerable to do," asserted Bart in a definite tone that instantly attracted his mother's attention because of its seriousness. "Father is a bonded employee of the express service. Their business doesn't stop because of an accidental fire, and they have a system to look after here that must not be neglected. I know the ropes pretty well, thanks to father, and I think it a matter of duty to act just as he would were he able to be about, and further and protect the company's interests. Outside of that, mother," continued the boy, earnestly, "you don't suppose I am going to sit down idly and let things drift at haphazard, with the family to take care of and everything to be done to make it easy and comfortable for father."

A look of pride came into the mother's face. She completely recognized the fidelity and sense of her loyal son, allowed Bart to lead her into the house, and tried to be calm and cheerful when he bade her good-bye, and, evading celebrating groups of his boy friends, made his way down to the ruined express shed.

A heap of still smouldering cinders and ashes marked the site. Bart stood silently ruminating for some minutes. He tried to think things out clearly, to decide how far he was warranted in acting for his father.

"I don't exactly know what action the express people usually take in a case of this kind," he reflected, "nor how soon they get about it. I can only wait for some official information. In the meantime, though, somebody has got to keep the ball rolling here. I seem to be the only one about, and I am going to put the system in some temporary order at least. If I'm called down later for being too officious, they can't say I didn't try to do my duty."

Bart set briskly at work to put into motion a plan his quick, sensible mind had suggested.

About one hundred feet away was a rough unpainted shed-like structure. He remembered the time, several years back, when the express office had been located there.

It was, however, forty feet from any tracks, and for convenience sake, when the railroad gave up the burned building which they had occupied for unclaimed freight storage, it had been turned over to the express people.

Bart went down to the old quarters. The door had lost its padlock and stood half open. Inside was a heap of old boards, and empty boxes and barrels thrown there from time to time to keep them from littering the yards.

A truck and the little delivery cart, being outside of the burned shed, Bart found intact. He ran them down to the building he had determined to utilize, temporarily at least, as express headquarters for Pleasantville.

The yards were fairly deserted except for a sleepy night watchman here and there. It was not yet seven o'clock, but when Bart reached the in-freight house he found it open and one or two clerks hurrying through their work so as to get off for the day at ten.

There was a good deal of questioning, for they knew of the fire, and knew Bart as well, and liked him, and when he made his wants known willing hands ministered to his needs.

Bart carried back with him a hammer and some nails, a broom, a marking pot and brush, pens, ink and a couple of tabs of paper.

As he neared the switch shanty where Lem Wacker had been on duty the day previous, he noticed that it had been opened up since he had passed it last. Some one was grumbling noisily inside. Bart was curious for more reasons than one.

He placed his load on the bench outside and stuck his head in through the open doorway.

"Oh, it's you, Mr. Evans," he hailed, as he recognized the regular flagman on duty for whom Wacker had been substituting for three days past. "Glad to see you back. Are you all well?"

"Eh? oh, young Stirling. Say, you've had a fire. I hear your father was burned."

"He is quite seriously hurt," answered Bart gravely.

"Too bad. I have troubles of my own, though."

"What is the matter, Mr. Evans?"

"Next time I give that lazy, good-for-nothing Lem Wacker work he'll know it, I'm thinking! Look there—and there!"

The irate old railroader kicked over the wooden cuspidor in disgust. It was loaded to the top with tobacco and cigarette ends. Then he cast out half a dozen empty bottles through the open window, and went on with his grumbling.

"What he's been up to is more than I can guess," he vociferated. "Look at my table there, all burned with matches and covered with burnt cork. What's he been doing with burnt cork? Running a minstrel show?"

Bart gave a start. He thought instantly of the black streaked face he had tried to survey at the express shed window the night previous.

Bart Stirling's Road to Success

"My flag's gone, too," muttered old Evans, turning over things in a vain search for it. "I'll have a word or two for Lem Wacker when it comes to settling day, I'm thinking. He comes up to the house late last night and tells me he don't care to work for me any longer."

"Did he?" murmured Bart thoughtfully. "Why not, I wonder?"

"Oh, he flared up big and lofty, and said he had a better job in view."

Bart went on his way surmising a good deal and suspecting more.

He made it a point to pass by the ruins of the old express shed, and he found there what he expected to find—the missing flag from the switch shanty; only the rod was bare, the little piece of red bunting having been burned away.

Bart dismissed this matter from his mind and all other disturbing extraneous affairs, massing all his faculties for the time being on getting properly equipped for business.

He selected a clean, plain board, and with the marking outfit painted across it in six-inch letters that could be plainly read at a distance the words:

EXPRESS OFFICE.

This Bart nailed to the door jamb in such a way that it was visible from three directions.

Next he started to carry outside and pile neatly at the blind end of the building all the boards, boxes and other debris littering up the room, swept it, and selected two packing cases and nailed them up into a convenient impromptu desk, manufactured a bench seat out of some loose boards, set his pen, ink and paper in order, and felt quite ready for business.

He had gained a pretty clear idea the day previous from his father as to the Fourth of July express service routine.

The fireworks deliveries had been the main thing, but as these had been destroyed that part of the programme was off the sheet.

At eight o'clock the morning express would bring in its usual quota, but this would be held over until the following day except what was marked special or perishable. There would be no out express matter owing to the fact that it was a holiday.

"I can manage nicely, I think," Bart told himself, as, an hour later, he ran the truck down to the site of the burned express shed and stood by the tracks waiting.

A freight engine soon came to the spot, backing down the express car. Its engineer halted with a jerk and a vivid:

"Hello!"

He had not heard of the fire, and he stared with interest at the ruins as Bart explained that, until some new arrangement was made, express shipments would be accepted and loaded by truck.

There were four big freezers of ice cream, one for delivery at the town confectioner's, one at the drug store soda fountain, and two for the picnic grounds, where an afternoon celebration was on the programme. Besides these, there were three packages containing flags and fireworks, marked "Delayed—Rush."

He closed the office door, tacked to it a card announcing he would return inside of half an hour, and loaded into the wagon the entire morning's freight except the two freezers intended for the picnic grounds.

These could not be delivered until two o'clock that afternoon, and he stowed them in the new express shed, covering them carefully with their canvas wrappings.

Bart made a record run in his deliveries. He had formed a rough receipt book out of some loose sheets, and when he came back to the office filled out his entries in regular form.

Several persons visited the place up to nine o'clock—storekeepers and others who had lost their goods in the fire. Bart explained the situation, saying that they would probably hear from the express company in a day or two regarding their claims.

He found in work something to change his thoughts from a gloomy channel, and, while very anxious about his father, was thankful his parent had escaped with his life, while he indulged some hopeful and daring plans for his own ambitions in the near future.

"I'll stick to my post," he decided. "Some of the express people may happen down here any time."

He was making up a list from memory of those in the village whose packages had been destroyed by the fire, when two boys crossed the threshold of the open doorway, one carrying a thin flat package.

Bart greeted them pleasantly. The elder was Darry Haven, his companion a younger brother, Bob, both warm friends of the young express agent.

Darry inquired for Mr. Stirling solicitously, and said his mother was then on her way to see Mrs. Stirling, anxious to do anything she could to share the lady's troubles. Mr. Haven had been an editor, but his health had failed, and Mrs. Haven, having some artistic ability and experience, was the main present support of the family, doing considerable work for a publishing house in the city in the way of illustrations for fashion pages.

Darry had a "rush" package of illustrations under his arm now.

"I suppose we can't get anything through to-day, or until you get things in running order again?" he intimated.

"We were sending nothing through on account of the Fourth," explained Bart, "but you leave the package here and I will see that it goes on the eleven o'clock train."

Bart had just completed the fire-loss list when a heavy step caused him to turn around.

A portly, well-dressed man, important-appearing and evidently on business, stood in the doorway looking sharply about the place.

"Well!" he uttered, "What's this?"

"The express office," said Bart, arising.

"Oh, it is?" slowly commented the man, "You in charge?"

"Yes, sir," politely answered Bart.

"Set up shop; doing business, eh?"

"Fast as I can," announced Bart.

"Who told you to?" demanded the visitor bending a pair of stern eyes on Bart.

"Why do you ask that, may I inquire?" interrogated Bart, pleasantly, but standing his ground.

"Ha-hum!" retorted the stranger, "why do ask. Because I am the superintendent of the express company, young man, and somewhat interested in knowing, I fancy!"

CHAPTER VI

GETTING "SATISFACTION"

Bart did not lose his presence of mind, but he fully realized that he faced a critical moment in his career.

Very courteously he drew forward the rude impromptu bench he had knocked together two hours before.

"Will you have a seat, sir?" he asked.

The express superintendent did not lose his dignity, but there was a slightly humorous twitching at the corners of his mouth.

"Thanks," he said, wearily seating himself on the rude structure. "Rather primitive furniture for a big express company, it seems to me."

"It was the best I could provide under the circumstances," explained Bart modestly.

"You made this bench, did you?"

Bart acknowledged the imputation with a nod.

"And that—desk, is it?"

"Yes, sir."

"And the sign outside, and opened for business?"

"There was no one else on hand. I felt that I must represent my father, Mr. Stirling, who is the authorized agent here, until the seriousness of his condition was known. You see, there was business likely to come in, and I have been here to attend to it."

"Just so," vouchsafed his visitor. "No out shipments to-day, I believe?"

"No, it's a holiday, but there was some rush in stuff on the morning express."

"Where is it?"

"I have delivered most of it—the balance, two freezers of ice cream, I will attend to this afternoon. I am keeping a record and taking receipts, but giving none—I didn't feel warranted in that until I heard from the company."

"You have done very well, young man," said the stranger. "I am Robert Leslie, the superintendent, as I told you. Do you mean to say you rigged things up in this shape and got your deliveries out alone?"

"There was no one to help me," remarked Bart.

He felt pleased and encouraged, for the superintendent's cast-iron visage had softened considerably, and he manifested unmistakable interest as he reached out and took up and inspected the neatly formulated memoranda on the packing-box desk.

"What's this?" he inquired, running over the pages Bart had last been working on.

"That is a list of losers by the fire," explained Bart.

"This is from memory?"

"Yes, Mr. Leslie—but I have a good one, and I think the list is tolerably correct."

"I am very much pleased," admitted the superintendent—"those claims are our main anxiety in a case like this. I understand the contents of the safe were destroyed."

"I fear so," assented Bart gravely. "The explosion was so sudden, and my father was blinded, so there was no opportunity to close it. I tried to reach it after rescuing him, but the flames drove me back."

Mr. Leslie was silent for a few moments. He seemed to be thinking. His glance roamed speculatively about the place, taking in the layout critically, then finally Bart was conscious that his shrewd, burrowing eyes were scanning him closely.

"How old are you, Stirling?" asked the superintendent abruptly.

"Nearly nineteen."

"I suppose you know something about the routine here?"

"I have helped my father a little for the past month or two—yes, sir."

"And have improved your opportunities, judging from the common-sense way you have got things into temporary running order," commented Leslie.

The speaker took out his watch. Then, glancing through the doorway, he arose suddenly, with the words:

"Ah! there he is, now. I suppose you couldn't be here about four o'clock this afternoon?"

"Why, certainly," answered Bart promptly. "People are likely to be around making inquiries, and I have a delivery to make this afternoon, as I told you, sir."

"I intend to see your father," said Mr. Leslie, "and I want to get back to the city to-night. I may have some orders for you, so we'll call it four, sharp."

"I will be here, sir."

The superintendent stepped outside. Evidently he had made an appointment, for he was met by the freight agent of the B. & M., who knew Bart and nodded to him.

As the two men strolled slowly over to the ruins of the express shed, Bart heard Mr. Leslie remark:

"That's a smart boy in there."

"And a good one," supplemented the freight agent.

Bart experienced a thrill of pleasure at the homely compliment. He tried to get back to business, but he found himself considerably flustered.

All the morning his hopes and plans had drifted in one definite direction—to get some assurance of permanent employment for the future.

The only work he had ever done was here at the express office for his father. It was a daring prospect to imagine that he, a mere boy, would be allowed to succeed to a grown man's position and salary—and yet Bart had placed himself in line for it with every prompting of diligence and duty.

Mr. Leslie and the freight agent spent half an hour at the ruins. Bart could see by their gestures that they were animatedly discussing the situation, and they seemed to be closely looking over the ground with a view to locating a site for a new express shed.

Finally they shook hands in parting. The express superintendent consulted his watch, and turned his face in the direction of Bart.

As he neared the "new" express shed, however, he passed around to its rear, and glancing out of a window there Bart saw that he had come to a halt, and was drawing a diagram of the tracks on a blank page in his memorandum book.

Just as Mr. Leslie had returned this to his pocket and was about to start from the spot, a man hailed him. It was Lem Wacker. He was dressed in his best, but the effort was spoiled by an uncertainty of gait, and his face was suspiciously flushed.

"Did you address me?" inquired the superintendent in a chilling tone.

Lem was not daunted by the imposing presence or the dignified demeanor of the speaker.

"Sure," he answered, unabashed. "You're Leslie, ain't you?"

"I am Mr. Leslie, yes," corrected the superintendent, his stern brow contracted in a frown.

"They told me I'd find you here. My name's Wacker. Knew your cousin down at Rochelle; we worked on the same desk in the freight house. Had many a drink with Ted Leslie."

"What do you want?" challenged the superintendent, turning on his heel.

"Why, it's this way," explained the dauntless Lem: "I'm an old railroader and a handy man of experience, I am, and I wanted to make a proposition to you. You see—"

Bart lost the remainder of Mr. Lem Wacker's proposition, for Mr. Leslie had started forward impatiently, with Lem persistently following in his wake. He was still keeping up the pursuit and importuning the affronted official as both were lost to view behind a track of freights.

Bart of course surmised that Lem Wacker was on the trail of the "better job" he had announced he was after to the old switchman, Evans.

"I don't think he has made a very promising impression," decided Bart, as he got back to his writing.

"Say, you!"

Bart looked up a trifle startled at the sharp hail, ten minutes later. He had been engrossed in his work and had not noticed an intruder.

Lem Wacker stood just in the doorway. He looked flushed, excited and vicious.

"What can I do for you, Mr. Wacker?" inquired Bart calmly, though scenting trouble in the air.

"You can undo!" flared out Wacker, "and you'll get quick action on it, or I'll clean you out, bag and baggage."

"There isn't much baggage here to clean out," suggested Bart humorously, "and as for the rest of it I'll try to take care of it myself."

"Oh! you will, will you?" sneered Lem, lurching to and fro. "You're a sneak. Bart Stirling—a low, contemptible sneak, that's what you are!"

"I would like to have you explain," remarked Bart.

"You've queered me!" roared Wacker, "and I'm going to have satisfaction—yes, sir. Sat-is-fac-tion!"

He pounded out the syllables under Bart's very nose with resounding thumps, bringing down his fist on the impromptu office desk so forcibly that the concussion disturbed the papers on it, and several sheets fell fluttering to the floor.

Bart's patience was tried. His eyes flashed, but he stooped and picked up the pages and replaced them on the dry goods box.

"Don't you do that again," he warned in a strained tone.

"Why!" yelled Wacker, rolling up his cuffs.

"I'll trim you next! 'Don't-do-it-again!' eh? Boo! bah!"

Lem raised his foot and kicked over the desk, papers and all.

"That's express company property," observed Bart quietly, but his blood was up, the limit reached. "Get out!"

One arm shot forward, and the clenched muscular fist rested directly under the chin of the astounded Lem Wacker.

"And stay out."

Lem Wacker felt a smart whack, went whirling back over the threshold, and the next instant measured his length, sprawling on the ground outside of the express shed.

CHAPTER VII

WAITING FOR TROUBLE

Lem Wacker rolled over, then sat up, rubbed his head in a half-dazed manner, and muttered in a silly, sheepish way.

"Lem Wacker," said Bart, "I have got just a few words to say to you, and that ends matters between us. I am sorry I had to strike you, but I will have no man interfering with the express company's affairs. I want you to go away, and if you ever come in here again except on business strictly there will be trouble."

Lem did not put up much of a belligerent front, though he tried still to look ugly and dangerous.

He got his balance at last, and extended his finger at our hero.

"Bart Stirling," he maundered, "you've made an enemy for life. Look out for me! You're a marked man after this."

"What am I marked with," inquired Bart quickly—"burnt cork?"

"Hey! What?" blurted out Lem, and Bart saw that the shot had struck the target. Wacker looked sickly, and muttered something to himself. Then he took himself off.

Bart's worries were pleasantly broken in upon by the arrival of his sister Bertha. She brought him a generous lunch, the first food Bart had tasted that day, and his appetite welcomed it in a wholesome way.

He put in the time planning what he would do if he was lucky enough to be retained in his father's position, and what he might do in case someone else was appointed.

At half-past two Bart loaded the two ice cream freezers on the cart and started for the picnic grounds.

Juvenile Pleasantville had somewhat subsided for a time in the fervor of its patriotism. There was a lull in the popping and banging, nearly everybody in town being due at the time-honored celebration in the picnic grove.

When Bart reached the grove, someone was making an address, and he piloted his way circumspectly up to the side of the platform where the speaking was going on.

He deposited the freezers inside the bunting-decorated inclosure, where half a dozen young ladies were posted to dispense the refreshments after the literary programme was finished.

Bart started to return with his empty cart the way he had come, but about ten feet from the platform paused for a moment to take in the exceptionally flowery sentiment that was being enunciated by the speaker of the day.

Colonel Harrington, it seemed, was the self-appointed hero of the occasion. The great man of the village was in his element—the eyes and ears of all Pleasantville fixed upon him.

In rolling tones and with magnificent gestures he was paying a lofty tribute to the immortal Stars and Stripes waving just over his head, when, his eyes lowering, they focused straight in a fixed stare on Bart.

The colonel gave the young express agent an awful look, and in an instant Bart knew that the military man had been informed of the identity of the audacious cannoneer of the evening previous.

Like some orators, the colonel, once disturbed by an extraneous contemplation, lost his voice, cue and self-possession all in a second.

It seemed as if he could not take his eyes from the innocent and embarrassed author of his distraction.

He spluttered, the rounded sentence on his lips died down to measly insignificance, he stammered, stumbled, and sat down with a red face, his eyes darting rage at poor Bart.

Some of the boys in the crowd "caught on" to the situation, and giggled and made significant remarks, but the chairman on the platform covered the colonel's confusion by announcing the national anthem, and Bart effected his escape.

"He'll never forgive me, now," decided Bart. "The damage to the statue was bad enough, but breaking him up as my appearance did just now is the limit. I hope Mr. Leslie doesn't hear of my unfortunate escapade, and I hope the colonel doesn't undertake to hurt my chances. He's an irrational firebrand when he takes a dislike to anybody, and Mrs. Harrington is worse."

Bart had a foundation for this double criticism. The colonel was a pompous, self-important individual, intensely selfish and domineering, and his wife a thoughtless devotee of fashion and society.

Mrs. Stirling did some very fine fancy work, and a few months previous to the opening of this tale the magnate's wife had asked as a favor that she embroider some handkerchiefs as a wedding present for a relative.

She never visited the Stirling house but she left some sting or sneer of affected superiority behind her, and when the work was done took it home, and the next day sent a note complaining that the handkerchiefs were spoiled, inclosing about one-fifth the usual compensation for such labor. But she did not return the handkerchiefs.

Mrs. Stirling later learned that their recipient had expressed herself perfectly delighted with the delicate, beautiful gift, but, being a true lady, Bart's mother said nothing about the matter to those who would have been glad to spread a little gossip unfavorable to the dowdy society queen of Pleasantville.

The village hardware store was open for the sale of powder, and Bart stopped there on his way back to the express office and purchased a padlock, two keys fitting it, and some stout staples and a hasp. He carried these articles into the office when he reached it.

The thoughts of his father's plight, a haunting dread that Colonel Harrington might make him some trouble, and the uncertainty of continued work in the express service, all combined to depress his mind with anxiety and suspense, and he tried to dismiss the themes by whistling a quiet, soothing tune as he started to get the hammer to put the padlock in place.

The minute he opened the door, however, the whistle was instantly checked, and a quick glance at the impromptu desk told Bart that the place had welcomed a visitor since he had left it.

On a sheet of blank paper was scrawled the words: "Express safe was locked last night—contents all right."

And beside it was a heap of account books—the entire records of the office, which Bart had supposed were destroyed in the fire at the old express shed the evening previous.

CHAPTER VIII

THE YOUNG EXPRESS AGENT

Our hero regarded the little pile of account books as if they represented some long-lost, newly-found treasure.

He was very much astonished at their presence there. They were a tangible reality, however, and no delusion of the senses, and his ready mind took in the fact that someone had in an unaccountable manner rescued them from the burning express shed, and mysteriously restored them to the proper representative of the express company in the nature of a vast surprise.

The edges of one of the books was scorched, which was the only evidence that they had been in the flames.

They were all there, and Bart was very glad. He now had in his possession every record of the transactions of the Pleasantville express office since the last New Year's day.

"And the contents of the safe are all right, too, that writing says!" exclaimed Bart; "now what does all this mean?"

The handwriting of the announcement was crude and labored, and the boy felt sure he had never seen it before.

He glanced with some excitement at the ruins of the old express shed, then he went over there. The embers had died down entirely, and the mass of ashes and debris was sparkless and cold.

Bart went to a near railroad scrap heap and selected a long iron rod crowbar crooked at the end. He returned to the ruins and began poking the debris aside. He was thus engaged when some trackmen, lounging the day away over on a freight platform, sauntered up to the spot.

"Why don't you work holidays, Stirling?" asked one of them satirically.

"Somebody has got to work to get this mess in shipshape order," retorted Bart. "The writing said what was true!" he spoke to himself, as his pokings cleared a broad iron surface. "The safe door is shut."

The safe lay flat on its back where it had fallen when the floor had burned away. It was an old-fashioned affair with a simple combination attachment, and so far as Bart could make out had suffered no damage beyond having its coat of lacquer and gilt lettering burned off.

He leaned over and felt of its surface, which retained scarcely any heat now.

"We heard the old iron box was caught open by the fire and everything in it burned up," spoke one of the trackmen.

"I supposed so myself," said Bart, "but it seems otherwise. I wonder how heavy it is?"

"Wait till I get some tackle," said one of the workmen.

He went away and returned with two crowbars and a pulley and block tackle.

It was no work at all for those stout, experienced fellows to get the safe clear of the ruins, and, with the aid of a big truck they brought from the freight house, convey it to the new express quarters.

Just as the town bell rang out four o'clock, Mr. Leslie stepped over the threshold.

He glanced about the place briskly, gave a start as he noticed the heap of account books at Bart's elbow, and looked both pleased and puzzled as his eyes lighted on the safe.

"Why, Stirling!" he exclaimed, "are you a wizard?"

"Not quite," replied Bart with a smile, "but someone else seems to be."

"Are those the office books we thought burned up, and the safe?"

"Yes, sir."

"How is this?"

Bart told of the mysterious return of the books and of the scrap of writing that had led him to dig up the safe.

"That's a pretty strange circumstance," observed Mr. Leslie thoughtfully. "How do you account for it?"

Bart Stirling's Road to Success

"I can't," admitted Bart, "except to theorize, of course, that someone had enough interest in myself or the company to rush into the burning shed and save the books and close the safe while I was getting my father to safety."

"That's rational, but who was it?" persisted Mr. Leslie.

"Whoever it was," said Bart, "he has certainly proved himself a good, true friend."

"Have you no idea who it is?" challenged Mr. Leslie sharply.

Bart hesitated for a moment.

"Why, yes," he admitted finally. "I am pretty sure who it is. I do not know his name, but I have seen him several times," and Bart thought it best to reveal to his superior all he knew about the roustabout who had warned him of the burglary, who had assisted him in rescuing his father from the burning express shed, and who had vanished suddenly as people began to crowd to the scene of the blaze.

"I would like to meet that man!" commented Mr. Leslie.

"I hardly think that possible," explained Bart. "He seems to be afraid to face the open daylight, and, as you see, has not even manifested himself to me, except in a covert way."

"He is some poor unfortunate in trouble," said the superintendent. "If you do see him, Stirling, give him that—from the express company."

Bart was sure that his mysterious friend could be no other than the roustabout. He took the crisp ten-dollar bill, which the superintendent extended with an impetuousness that showed he was a genuine, warm-hearted man under the surface.

"That quarter of a dollar you gave him was a grand investment, Stirling. And now to get down to business, for I haven't much time to spare."

The superintendent, seating himself on the bench, consulted his watch and fixed his glance on Bart in his former stern, practical way.

"I saw your father at the hospital," he announced.

"Yes, sir?" murmured Bart anxiously.

"They are going to let him go home to-morrow. I am very sorry for his misfortune. He is an old and reliable employee of the express company, and we will find it difficult to replace him. I have thought over a suggestion he made, and have decided to offer you his position."

"Oh, sir! I thank you," said Bart spontaneously, and the tears of gladness and pride sprang to his eyes uncontrollably.

"Technically your father will appear in our service. I do not think the company bonding him will refuse to continue to be his surety. You must make your own arrangement as to legally representing him, signing his name and the like, and of course you will have to do all the work, for he will be helpless for some time to come. Are you willing to undertake the responsibility?"

"Gladly."

"Then that is settled. This arrangement will be in force for sixty days. If, at the end of that time your father is no better, I do not doubt that we will give you the regular appointment, if in the meantime you fill the bill acceptably."

"I shall do my best."

"And I believe you will succeed. I like you, Stirling," said Mr. Leslie frankly, "and I am greatly pleased at the way you have stood in the breach at a critical time, and protected the company's interests. You will continue to draw fifty-five dollars a month, and use your judgment in incurring any expense necessary to keep things running smoothly until we get a new express office built. What is in the safe?"

Bart was familiar with its contents. He itemized them, including some fifty unclaimed parcels of small bulk that had accumulated during the year.

"Get rid of all that stuff," ordered the superintendent briskly. "I shall advise all the small offices in this division to ship in all their uncalled-for matter. Advertise a sale, make your returns to the company, and start with a new sheet. I think that is all there is any need of discussing at present, but I will send instructions by wire or mail as the occasion comes up. Count me your friend as long as you show the true manhood you have displayed to-day in a situation that would have rattled and frightened most boys—and grown men, too. Good-by."

He was keen, practical business to the core, and no sentiment about him, for he arose promptly with the farewell words, shook hands with Bart in an off-hand way, and was gone like a flash to catch his train to the city.

Bart stood for a moment in a kind of daze. The congratulatory words of the superintendent, and the appointment to the position of agent, stirred the dearest desires of his heart.

His great good fortune momentarily overwhelmed him, and he stood staring silently after the superintendent in a grand dream of opulence and ambition.

"I want you!" spoke a harsh, sudden voice, and Bart Stirling came out of dreamland with a shock.

CHAPTER IX

COLONEL JEPTHA HARRINGTON

The young express agent recognized the tones before he saw the speaker's face. Only one person in Pleasantville had that mixture of lofty command and tragic emphasis, and that was Colonel Jeptha Harrington.

As Bart turned, he saw the village magnate ten feet away, planted like a rock, and extending his big golden-headed cane as if it was a spear and he was poising to immediately impale a victim. The colonel's brow was a veritable thundercloud.

"Yes, sir," announced Bart promptly—"what can I do for you?"

Bart did not get excited in the least. He looked so cool and collected that the colonel ground his teeth, stamped his foot and advanced swinging his cane alarmingly.

"I've come to see you—" he began, and choked on the words.

"May I ask what for?" interrogated Bart.

Colonel Harrington shook, as he placed his cane under his arm and took out his big plethoric wallet.

He selected a strip of paper and held it between his forefinger and thumb.

"Young man," he observed, "do you know what that is?"

Bart shook his head.

"Well, I'll tell you, it's a bill, do you hear? a bill. It's for eighty-five dollars, damage done maliciously on my private grounds, yesterday evening. It represents the bare cost of a new copper pedestal to replace the one you shot to pieces last night, and it's a wonder you are not in jail for murder, for had that cannon ball struck a human being—Enough! before I take up this outrage with the district attorney in its criminal phase, are you going to settle the damage, or are you not?"

"Colonel Harrington, I haven't got eighty-five dollars."

"Then get it!" snapped the Colonel.

"Nor can I get it."

"Then," observed the colonel, restoring the bit of paper to his pocket—"go to jail!"

Bart regarded his enemy dumbly. Colonel Harrington was a power in Pleasantville, his will and his way were paramount there.

"I am sorry," said Bart finally, in a tone of genuine distress, "but eighty-five dollars is a sheer impossibility—in cash. If you would listen to me—"

"But I shan't!"

"I would like to offer payment or replace the pedestal on reasonable terms."

"It don't go!"

"And, further, I am not to blame in the matter."

"What!" roared the colonel "what's that?"

"It's the truth," asserted Bart. "I never knew the cannon was loaded with a ball."

"Do you know who loaded it?"

Bart was silent.

"You won't tell? We'll see if a jury can't make you, then!" fumed the colonel. "Aha! it's serious now, is it? Not so much fun breaking up my home and breaking up my speech at the grove to-day, hey?"

Bart saw very plainly that what rankled most with his volcanic visitor was the blow to his pride he had suffered that afternoon at the grove.

"You put me in a nice fix, didn't you?" cried the colonel—"laughing stock of the community! Young man, you're on the downward road, fast. You're all of a brood. Your mother—"

Bart started forward with a dangerous sparkle in his eye.

"Colonel Harrington," he said decisively, "my mother has nothing to do with this affair."

"She has!" vociferated the magnate, "or rather, her teachings. You're full of infernal pride and presumption, the whole kit of you!"

"We have our rights."

"I'm a stockholder in the B. & M., and I fancy my influence will reach the express service. You'll stay in your present job just long enough for me to advise your employers of your true character."

Bart was dismayed—that threat touched him to the quick. He had felt very glad that Mr. Leslie had not met the irate colonel. The mean-spirited magnate noted instantly the effect of his threat.

"You'll insult and defy me, will you?" he cried, with a gloating chuckle. "Very well—you take your medicine, that's all."

Bart could hardly control his voice, but he said simply:

"Colonel Harrington, my father has been blinded at his post of duty. I am the sole support of the family. I hope you will pause and consider before you plunge us into new trouble and distress that we do not deserve. I have never had the remotest thought of injuring you or your property in any way. I am willing to make all the amends I am able for the accidental damage to your property, but I can't and won't cringe to your injustice, nor grovel at your feet."

"Eighty-five dollars—one, the name of the person who loaded that cannon—two, C.O.D. before ten o'clock to-morrow morning, or I'll sweep you off the map!" shouted the colonel.

He marched off, puffing up as his vain senses were tickled with the fancy that he was a born orator, and had just given utterance to some profoundly apt and clever sentiments. Bart stared after him in sheer dismay.

"It's a bad outlook," he murmured, "but—I have tried to do my duty. I would like to have money and influence, but would rather be plain Bart Stirling than that man. He is coming back."

Bart thought this, for, just about to round the end of a dead freight and cross to the public street, his late visitor turned abruptly.

He did not, however, retrace his steps. Instead, he came to the strangest rigid pose Bart had ever seen a human being assume.

He stood staring, spellbound, at the partly open door of the nearest freight car. His cane had fallen from his hand, his head was thrown up as if he had been struck a stunning blow under the chin, and even at the distance he was, Bart could see that his usually red-puffed face was the color of chalk. Almost immediately, through the open doorway space of the freight car an arm was protruded.

Its index finger was pointed, inflexible as an iron rod, directly at the colonel. It fascinated and transfixed the military man, and Bart Stirling, staring also at the strange tableau, was overcome with perplexity and mystification.

CHAPTER X

QUEER COMRADES

So many sensational occurrences had marked the last twenty-four hours of Bart Stirling's career, that it seemed as though the accumulating series would never end.

It was a particularly ragged and miserable-looking arm, and why it could so summarily check, halt and hold the great magnate of Pleasantville, was the problem that now tried Bart's reasoning faculties.

Bart closed the door of the express office and stepped out to where he could get a clearer view of the colonel and his environment.

Suddenly the strain was removed. The colonel threw up his arms with a gasp. He started to turn around, clutched at his neck in a strangling kind of a way, tottered, reeled, and plunged forward on his face against a heap of cinders.

"This is serious," murmured Bart.

He rapidly covered the two hundred foot space between the express shed and the freight car.

"Colonel—Colonel Harrington!" he called in some alarm, kneeling by the prostrate body of his enemy.

Bart tried to pull him over on his back. As he partially succeeded, he noticed that the colonel's face was pitted, and in one or two places scratched and bleeding from contact with the cinder particles.

The bulky form was quivering and convulsed. The colonel had been dazed, it seemed, but not rendered entirely unconscious, for now with a groan he struggled to a sitting posture.

Bart drew out his handkerchief and tried to clean the dirt from the military man's face.

The colonel resisted, he swayed and mumbled. Then he groaned again as his eyes lit on the freight car.

"Get me away from here," he moaned—"get me away! What's happened to me?"

"That is what I was going to ask you," said Bart. "Don't you know?"

The colonel passed his hand over his face and mumbled, but made no coherent reply.

Bart glanced at the freight car. It afforded no evidence of present occupancy. He reflected for moment.

"Wait for just two minutes," he directed.

Running over to the drug store on the next street, he spoke a few words to the man in charge, and darted out again as the druggist hurried to his telephone to call up the livery stable.

When he got back to the colonel, Bart found the latter sitting propped up against the cinder heap, his eyes open, and breathing heavily, but still in a helpless kind of a daze.

He worked over the colonel, and finally got the man on his feet. His position was so unsteady, however, that he had to support him with one hand while he dusted off his clothes with the other.

As he stood trying to keep his charge on his feet, a cab rushed across the tracks. Its driver, bluff Bill Carey, nodded familiarly to Bart, and looked the colonel over critically. He got the latter into the cab in an experienced way.

"Same old complaint!" he intimated to Bart with a wink. "Drinks pretty heavily."

Bart leaned over into the cab.

"Colonel Harrington," he said, "do you wish to be driven home?"

The colonel gave him a fishy stare, groaned and put out a wavering hand.

"Come," he mumbled.

"Jump in," directed Carey. "You'll be useful explaining the 'fall' up at the house!"

As they went on their way, the young express agent experienced a striking sensation.

A topsy-turvy day of excitement was ending with the peculiar combination of his riding in the same carriage with his most bitter enemy, and acting the good Samaritan.

They proceeded slowly, or rather cautiously, for the popping and banging had recommenced all over town.

Carey had to keep the spirited horses in strong check as they passed groups of boys, reckless of the quantity of firecrackers they deliberately fired off as the team neared them.

Suddenly the horses were pulled to their haunches with a vociferous shout. The cab swerved and creaked, and the horses' hoofs beat an alarming tattoo on the cobblestones.

"Whoa! whoa!" yelled Bill Carey. "You young villains! get that infernal machine out of the way. Can't you see—"

Bart stuck his head out of the cab window to view an animated scene.

A fourteen-inch cannon cracker was hissing and spitting out smoke barely two feet ahead of the terrified horses in the middle of the street.

At that moment it exploded. The horses gave a wild snort, a frightened jerk at the reins.

Bart saw the staunch driver dragged from his seat. He lit on his feet, braced, but was pulled over, as, with a fierce tug, the horses snapped the line in two.

Then, unrestrained, the team shot down the street without guide or hindrance and with the speed of the wind.

CHAPTER XI

"FORGET IT!"

The young express agent acted quickly. A single glance told him that the driver of the cab could do nothing.

The frightened horses were speeding ahead at a furious rate, could not be overtaken, and Bart doubted if anyone could stop them.

No one tried, but all got out of the way promptly as the team went tearing along. The horses came to a crossing, and, terrified anew at a spitting "Vesuvius" ahead, abruptly veered and turned down a side lane.

It was at this moment that Bart threw open the door of the cab, grasped a handle at the side of the vehicle, and drew himself up to the driver's seat.

The swing the horses made just then sent his feet flying out in a wild circle, but he held on, and the rebound landed him on the seat.

Our hero cast a quick look within the vehicle. The colonel had "rousted" up somewhat. Buffeted from side to side by the erratic and violent movements of the horses, he was trying to maintain his balance by frantically clinging with both hands to the cushion under him.

As a wheel struck a stone the jar drove him forward. His head smashed out the front glass, and he uttered a yell of fear.

"Don't stir—don't jump!" shouted Bart through the opening thus made.

"We'll be killed!" cried the man.

"No, we won't. Do as I say. I'm on deck, and I'll—"

Bart sized up the situation, counted its risks and possibilities, and described a sudden forward leap.

The lines were torn and trailing under the horses' feet. He cut the air in a reckless, but well planned dive.

Bart Stirling's Road to Success

Bart landed sprawling between the two horses, his knee striking the carriage pole.

Bracing himself there, he caught out at the head of either horse. With a firm grip his fingers closed on the bridle reins.

Ahead was a stony wagon track lining a deep gravel pit dangerously near its edge.

About a hundred feet further on ran the creek, sunk between banks some fifteen feet high.

Bart drew the bridles taut. He feared the tremendous strain would break them. The heads of the horses were now held as in a vice, but they snorted and continued to plunge forward with undiminished speed.

As a wheel landed in a rut full of thick mud, their pace was momentarily retarded. Bart jerked at the bridles. The horses paused fully, but pranced and backed.

"Jump—crawl out—quick, now!" shouted Bart breathlessly to the occupant of the cab.

The colonel had been bouncing around, groaning and yelling ever since he had awakened to a realization of his desperate plight.

"Wait a minute!" he puffed. "Gently! Wait till I get out. Then you can go on," was his remarkable concession.

Bart saw the bulky body of the magnate fall, rather than step from the vehicle. He landed clumsily at the side of the road, rolled up like a ball, but unhurt.

He was so near to the grinding wheels of the vehicle and kicking hoofs of the horses that Bart relaxed the bridles.

Instantly the horses sprang forward again, but, once clear of the colonel's prostrate body, Bart focused his strength on a final mastery of the maddened steeds.

He drew the bridles at a sharp, taut slant that must have cut their mouths fearfully at the tenderest part, for they fairly screamed with pain and terror.

He succeeded in facing them sideways, ran their heads into some brush, vaulted over them, and, landing safely on his feet in front of them, grabbed them near the bits and held them snorting and trembling at a standstill.

Then he unshipped one of the lines and tied it around a sapling, stroked the horse's heads, and succeeded in quieting them down.

Going back to the road, he discerned Colonel Harrington sitting up rubbing his head and staring about abstractedly.

Farther away was a flying excited figure. Bart recognized the disenthroned cabman. They met where the colonel sat.

"All gone to smash, I suppose!" hailed Carey.

"No, a window broken, wheels scraped a little—nothing worse," reported Bart.

"Where is the team?" panted Carey.

Bart pointed and explained, and the cabman forged ahead with a gratified snort.

"You stuck till you landed 'em," applauded Carey. "Stirling, you're nerve all through!"

Bart went up to Colonel Harrington and the latter got on his feet. Bart could see that either the druggist's potion or his succeeding violent experience had quite restored the magnate to his original self. He nursed a slight abrasion on his chin, looked at Bart sheepishly, and then stepped over to a big bowlder and rested against it.

"Are you feeling all right now, Colonel Harrington?" asked Bart courteously.

"Me? Now? Ah yes! Quite—er—er—thank you."

Bart was somewhat astonished at the words and manner of his whilom enemy.

Colonel Harrington looked positively embarrassed. He would glance at Bart, start to speak, lower his eyes, and, turning pale as he seemed to remember, and turning red as he seemed to realize, would fumble at his watch fob, run his fingers through his hair and act flustered generally.

"The cab will be back in a few minutes," remarked Bart. "It was a pretty bad shaking up, but I hope you are none the worse for it. Good day, Colonel Harrington."

Bart turned to leave. He heard the colonel spluttering.

"Hold on," ordered the magnate. "I want to give you—I want to give you—some money," he observed.

"I can't take it, Colonel Harrington," said Bart definitely. "If I have been of service to you I am glad, but you will remember I was in the same danger as yourself, and quite anxious to save my own skin."

"Bosh! I mean—maybe," retorted the colonel, getting bombastic, and then humble.

"Well, put up your money, Colonel," advised Bart. "As I say, if I have been of service to you I am glad."

"You hold on!" ordered Colonel Harrington, as Bart again moved to leave the spot.

The speaker poked in his wallet and brought out a strip of paper, which Bart recognized as the one he had so menacingly waved in his face an hour previous at the express shed.

Colonel Harrington again poked about in his pockets till he found a pencil. With somewhat unsteady fingers he inscribed his name at the bottom of the paper, and handed it to Bart.

"You take that," he directed.

"Why, this is a receipted bill for the damage done to your statue," said Bart.

"Eighty-five dollars—just so."

"But I haven't paid it!"

"You needn't. Serious mistake—I see that," said the colonel. "That is, I see it now. Satisified you didn't mean any harm. Sick of whole muddle. And about getting you discharged and all that rot—didn't mean it. Forget it! Was a little mad and excited; see!"

"I can't take your receipt for what I haven't paid, and what I am willing to pay as fast as I can," said Bart.

Bart Stirling's Road to Success

"Then tear it up—I won't take a cent!" declared Colonel Harrington obstinately.

"The cab is coming," remarked Bart. "Shall Mr. Carey drive you home?"

"Yes, I suppose so. Come here, quick!"

He grabbed Bart's arm and drew our hero close up to him, as though he had some pressing intelligence to impart before the cab interrupted.

"Forget it!" he whispered hoarsely.

"About the statue—I'll be glad to," said Bart frankly.

"No—no, the—the—"

"Runaway? I shall not mention it, Colonel Harrington."

The colonel released Bart's arm, but with a desperate groan. It was evident he was not fully satisfied.

"Sure you'll forget It!" he persisted, very much perturbed. "I don't mean my abusing you, or the runaway, or—or—I mean I had an accident after I left you at the express office. Someone hailed me—but you know, you know!"

The colonel cast a penetrating look on Bart, who shook his head negatively.

"I don't know, Colonel," he declared.

"Oh, come, now!" croaked the colonel, making a ghastly attempt to give the statement the aspect of a joke. Honest, you didn't hear anyone call to me?"

"No," replied Bart.

The cab drove up and halted.

"Don't do any talking. Don't start any gossip about—about—of course you won't! I've got your word. You're a truthful, reliable boy, Stirling, and I—I respect you," stumbled on the colonel. "Mum's the word, and I'll—I'll make you no trouble, see?"

"Thank you, Colonel Harrington," said Bart in a queer tone.

The colonel again regarded him penetratingly, and then got into the cab. He took the trouble of leaning out and waving his hand as the vehicle started up. He smiled in a sickly way at Bart, and once made a movement as if inclined to get out and once more suggest to the young express agent that he "forget it."

"That man is scared half to death over something," reflected Bart, as he took a short cut to regain the express office.

CHAPTER XII

THE MYSTERIOUS MR. BAKER

The little express office looked good to Bart as its precincts again sheltered him.

Things appeared better and clearer to him now than at any time during the past twenty-four hours, and his heart warmed up as he put his papers and books in order, saw that the safe was secured, and decided to close up business for the day.

Doctor Griscom from the hospital had dropped in for a few moments, and brought some news that lifted something of a cloud from the heart of the young express agent.

"I do not want to hold out any false hopes," he told Bart, "but there is a bare possibility that your father may not become totally blind."

"That is blessed news!" cried Bart fervently.

"It is all a question of time, and after that of skill," continued the surgeon. "Your father must have absolute rest and cheerful, comfortable surroundings; above all, peace of mind. I shall watch his case, and when I see the first indication of the services of some skilled specialist being of benefit to him I will tell you. It will cost you some money, but I will do all I can to make the expert reasonable in his charges."

"Don't think of that," said Bart impetuously. "With such a hope in view I am willing to work my finger ends off!"

Bart was, therefore, in high spirits as he left the express office, padlocking the door securely.

He was anxious to get home and then to the hospital, to impart to his mother and father in turn the assurance that they had a bread-winner able to work and glad to do so for their benefit.

Amid the buoyancy of the relief from the continuous strain and troubles of the day, Bart was bent on a quick dash for home when he remembered something that changed his plan.

"The roustabout, the poor fellow that I've got the ten dollars for, the good fellow, if I don't mistake, who saved the books and the contents of the safe!" exclaimed Bart. "Actually, I had forgotten all about him for the moment."

Bart stood still thinking, looking around speculatively, his fingers mechanically touching the bank note in his pocket which Mr. Leslie had given him in trust.

He did not reflect long. He went at once to the freight car whence he had seen the ragged arm extended two hours previous, and looked in.

Back at one end were some broken grapevine crates, and it was dim and shadowy there, so he called out.

"Any one here?"

"Yes," came from the corner, and there was a rustling of straw.

"I guess I know who," said Bart. "Come out of that, my good friend, and show yourself," he continued heartily.

"What for?" propounded a gloomy, wavering voice.

"What for? that's good!" cried Bart. "Oh, I know who you are, if I don't know your name."

"Baker will do."

"All right, Mr. Baker, friend Baker, you're true blue and the best friend I ever had, and I want to shake hands with you, and slap you on the back, and—help you."

A timid, muffled figure shifted into full outline, but not into clear view, against the side of the car.

Bart took a step nearer. He promptly caught at one hand of the slouching figure. Then he regarded it in perplexity.

The roustabout held with his other hand a canvas bag on his head so that it concealed nearly his entire face.

"Why!" said Bart, reaching suddenly up and momentarily pulling the impromptu hood aside. "What's the matter now? Where is your beard and long head of hair?"

"Burned."

"False?"

"Yes."

"Then you were disguised?"

"I tried to be," was responded faintly.

Bart stood for a moment or two queerly regarding the roustabout.

"Mr. Baker," he said finally, "I am bound to respect any wish you may suggest, but I declare I can't understand you."

"Don't try to," advised the roustabout in a dreary way. "I'm not worth it."

"Oh, yes, you are."

"And it wouldn't do any good."

"It might. It must!" declared Bart staunchly, "See here, I want to ask you a few questions and then I want to give you some advice, or rather tender my very friendly services. Do you know what you have done for me to-day?"

"No. If I have done anything to help you I am glad of it. You have been a friend to me—the only friend I've found."

"I'll be a better one—that is, if you will let me," pledged Bart warmly. "You warned me about the burglars last night; you helped me save my father's life."

"Anybody would do what I have done."

"No one did but yourself, just the same. Don't be cynical—you're something of a hero, if you only knew it. It was you who went into the burning express shed and saved the account books and closed the safe door."

"Who says so?" muttered Baker.

"I say so, and you know it—don't you?"

Baker made no response.

"Do you know what all this means for me and my family?" went on Bart. "You have done for me something I can never pay you for, something I can never forget. You are true blue, Mr. Baker! That's the kind of a worthless good-for-nothing person you are, and I want to call you my friend! Hello, now what is the matter?"

The matter was that the roustabout was crying softly like a baby. Bart was infinitely touched.

"I don't know your secrets," continued Bart earnestly, "and I certainly shall not pry into them without your permission, but I want to repay your kindness in some way. I can't rest till I do. All I can do is to guess out that you are in some trouble, maybe hiding. Well, let me share your troubles, let me hide you in a more comfortable way than lounging around cold freight cars with half enough to eat. You've done something grand in the last twenty-four hours—don't lose sight of that in mourning over your sins, if you have any, or in running away from some shadow that scares you. I'm not the only one who thinks you're a hero, either. There's someone else."

"Is there?" murmured the roustabout weakly.

"There is. It is Mr. Leslie, the express superintendent. I told him about you. He left this ten dollars for you, and the way he did it ought to make you proud."

Bart forced the bank note into Baker's hand. The man was shaking like a leaf from emotion. He stood like one spellbound, unable to take in all at once the good that was said of him and done him.

"Come," rallied Bart, giving him a ringing slap on the shoulder, "brace up and be what you have proved yourself to be—a man!"

Baker started electrically. His tones showed some force as he said:

"All right—you've made me feel good. But you don't know a whole lot, and I can't tell you. You say you're my friend."

"You believe that I am, do you not?"

"Yes, I do, and that's why I don't want to drag you into any complications. This ten dollars is mine, isn't it?"

"Certainly."

"Will you spend it for me?"

"What do you mean?"

"I want you to give me a pencil and some paper, and I will write out a list of some things I want. You take it and the ten dollars and bring me the things here to-morrow. I want you to promise in the meantime, though, that if you come upon me unawares, or when I'm asleep, or under any circumstances whatever, you will turn your head away and not look at my face."

Bart was very much puzzled.

"I think I see how it is," he said after a brief period of reflection, "you are afraid of being recognized?"

"Think that if you want to, maybe you're right," returned Baker. "Anyway, I don't want to do anything or have you do anything that will mix you up in my troubles. My way is the safe way. Will you do what I ask?"

"Yes," answered Bart promptly. "Can't I get the things you want to-night?"

"I am afraid not, for most of the stores are closed."

"That's right. Well, then, let me make a suggestion: I have two keys to the new express office. I'll give you one. After dark, if you don't want to do it in daylight, go over and unlock the door. Pick out two or three dry-goods boxes from the heap behind the shed, carry them in and rig up any kind of private quarters you like at the far corner of the shed. I'll see that nobody disturbs you. In a couple of hours I will bring you a blanket from the house and a nice warm lunch, and you can be comfortable and safe. I will relock the door on you, and if you want to leave at any time you can unfasten a window and get out."

Baker did not reply. Bart heard him mumbling to himself as though debating the proposition submitted to him.

"I don't want to make you a lot of trouble," he finally faltered out.

"Of course you don't, and won't," asserted Bart—"you want to give me pleasure, though, don't you? So you do as I suggest, and I'll sleep a good deal sounder than if you didn't. Here's the key. I will be over to the express office about eight o'clock. Is it a bargain?"

"Yes," answered the strange man.

CHAPTER XIII

"HIGHER STILL!"

About eight o'clock that evening Bart came down to the express office carrying a lunch basket and a blanket, as he had promised his erratic friend, Mr. Baker.

The young express agent had spent a busy day, and the evening promised to continue to furnish plenty for him to do.

He had the infinite pleasure of seeing his mother's face brighten up magically, when he related sufficient to her of the day's experience to satisfy her that the revenue from the express business was secure.

She had received some intimation of this from her husband's lips an hour previous at the hospital, and said that Mr. Stirling was feeling relieved and hopeful over the visit of the express superintendent, and the prospects of Bart succeeding to his position.

Bart very much wished to visit his father at once, but Mrs. Stirling said he had quieted for the night, was in no pain or mental distress, and it might not be wise to disturb him.

Bart told his mother something about the roustabout and their friendly relations, and the bottle of hot coffee, home-made biscuit sandwiches, and half a pie were put up for Bart's pensioner with willing and grateful care.

Bart also took a shade lantern with him, and lighted it when he came to the express office. He found the padlock loose.

He glanced over to the far dim end of the place. Baker had built a regular cross-corner barricade of packing boxes, man-high.

Bart set the lantern on the bench and approached the roustabout's hide-out.

"Are you there, Mr. Baker?" he inquired.

"Yes, I did just as you told me to do," came the reply, but the speaker did not show himself.

"Well, here's a blanket. Can you make up a comfortable bed?"

"Oh, yes, I've got a broad board on a slant, and plenty of room."

Bart lifted over the lunch basket.

"There you are!" he said briskly—"now enjoy yourself, and don't take a single care about anything. Have you made out that list of things you want?"

"Yes, here it is," and Baker handed over a piece of paper inclosing the ten-dollar bill.

"I'll attend to this promptly," said Bart. "Supposing I look it over right here? There may be some things you have noted down I want to ask you about."

"Maybe you'd better," assented Baker.

Bart sat down near the lantern. The bit of paper was covered with crude handwriting, the same as that which had announced to him that afternoon that the contents of the safe in the old express shed ruins were safe.

The list was not a very long one, but it was not easy to fill.

Baker gave the measurements of a very cheap cotton suit and the size of a cap with a very deep peak. He also notated a green eye-shade, a pair of goggles, and the ingredients for making a dark brown face stain.

In addition to this he wanted a dark gray hair switch, and it was easy to discern that his main idea was to prepare an elaborate disguise.

"All right," reported Bart, as he finished reading the list. "I'll have the things here just as early in the morning as I can get them. I'm going to put out the lantern, but I will then hand it over to you with some matches. It has got a shade, and you can focus the rays so they will not show outside. Here are a couple of magazines—I brought them from the house."

"You're mighty kind," said the refugee. "Hold on. I want to tell you something. Of course you think I'm acting strange. Some day, though, if things come out right, I'll explain to you, and you will say I did just right. There's another thing: you may think from my actions I am some desperate character. I hope I may burn up right in this shed to-night if I'm not telling the truth when I say to you that I never touched a dishonored penny, never harmed a soul, never did a wrong thing knowingly."

"I have confidence in your word, Mr. Baker," said Bart simply.

"Thank you, I'll prove I deserve it yet," declared the strange man.

There was a spell of silence. Finally Bart decided to venture a question on a theme he was very curious about.

"Do you know Colonel Jeptha Harrington?" he asked suddenly.

"Hoo—eh?"

He had startled Baker—his incoherent mutterings persuaded Bart of this.

"Don't you want to tell?" continued Bart. "All right, only it was you who waved an arm at him from the freight car this afternoon, wasn't it, now?"

"Well, yes, it was," admitted Baker in a low tone.

"And you said something to him."

"Yes, I did. See here, I heard him calling you down and threatening you, for I slunk up to the shed here to see what he was up to. I'm interested in him, I am, and so are others. When I got back in hiding I spoke out, I told him something—something that made his crabbed old soul wizen up, something that scared the daylights out of him. He had a brother, once. He's dead, now. I said something that made this old rascal think his brother's ghost had come back to earth to haunt him."

"How could you do that?" inquired Bart, very much interested.

"Because I had certain knowledge. Don't ask any further. It will all come out, some day—the day I'm waiting and working for. You saw how he was affected. Well, I threatened things that laid him out flat if he dared to so much as place a straw in your path."

"I understand, now," said Bart.

He waited for a minute or two, hoping Baker would divulge something further, but he did not do so, and Bart said good night, secured the padlock on the outside, and left the place with a parting cheery direction to his strange pensioner to sleep soundly and rest well.

The little ones were in bed when Bart got home, but his mother and the girls were sitting on the porch. Pretty well tired out, Bart joined them, and they all sat watching the last of the display of fireworks over near the common.

"This has been a pretty dull Fourth for you, Bart," said his mother sympathizingly.

"It has been a very busy Fourth, mother," returned Bart cheerfully — "I might say a very hopeful, happy Fourth. Except for the anxiety about father, I think I should feel very grateful and contented."

A graceful rocket parted the air at a distance, followed by the delighted shouts of juvenile spectators.

"Upward and onward," murmured Mrs. Stirling, placing a tender, loving hand on Bart's shoulder.

A second rocket went whizzing up. It raced the other, outdistanced it, seemed bound for the furthest heights, never swerving from a true, straight line.

Then it broke grandly, sending a radiant glow across the clear, serene sky.

"That's my motto," said Bart, a touch of intense resolve in his tones — "higher still!"

CHAPTER XIV

MRS. HARRINGTON'S TRUNK

"Hey, there! Stirling."

Bart was busy at his desk in the express office, but turned quickly as he recognized the tones.

Trouble in the shape of Lem Wacker loomed up at the doorway.

"What is it?" asked Bart.

It was a week after the Fourth, and in all that time Bart had not seen anything of the man whom he secretly believed was responsible for the fire at the old express office.

"Who's the responsible party here?" demanded Lem, making a great ado over consulting a book he carried.

"I am."

"All right, then—I represent Martin & Company, pickle factory."

"Oh, you've found a job, have you," spoke Bart, forced to smile at the bombastic business air assumed by his visitor.

"I represent Martin & Company," came from Wacker, in a solemn, dignified way. "Inspector. We want a rebate on that bill of lading."

Lem removed a slip from his loose-leaf book and tendered it to Bart.

"What's the matter with it?" inquired Bart.

"Consignment short," announced Wacker.

Bart looked him squarely in the eyes. Wacker had made the announcement malignantly. His gaze dropped.

"I'm hired to stop the leaks," he mumbled, "and if this office is responsible for any of them I'm the man to find it out."

"Well, in the present instance your claim is sheer folly. I see you note here one hundred and fifty pounds shortage. What is your basis?"

"I weighed them myself."

Bart consulted his books. Then he turned again to Wacker.

"This consignment was shipped as nine hundred and fifty pounds," he said. "It weighed that at the start."

"That's what the shipping agent says, yes."

"And you claim eight hundred pounds?"

"Exactly."

"It was weighed up here when received—nine hundred and fifty pounds."

"Come off!" jeered Wacker. "Wasn't I an express agent once and don't I know the ropes? What receiving agent ever takes the trouble to re-weigh!"

"My father did—I always do," announced Bart flatly.

"Even if you did," persisted Wacker, "what little one-horse agent dares to dispute the big company's weight at the other end of the line?"

"Oh," observed Bart smoothly, "you think there is a sort of collusion, do you?"

"Yes, I do—I am an expert!"

"Sorry to disturb the profundity of your calculations, Mr. Wacker," said Bart quietly, "but in the present instance there could not possibly be any mistake. Our scales were burned up in the fire. The new ones have not yet arrived, and in the meantime, as a temporary accommodation, our weighing is done up at the in-freight platform by the official weigh master of the road. I fancy Martin & Company will accept that verification as final. Don't you think so, Mr. Wacker?"

Lem Wacker snatched the paper Bart returned to him with a positive growl.

"I'll catch you Smart-Alecks yet!" he muttered surlily.

"What are you so anxious to catch us for?" inquired Bart coolly.

"Never you mind—I'll get you!"

Lem Wacker had said that before, and as he backed away Bart dismissed him with a shrug of his shoulders.

There were too many practical things occupying his time to waste any on fancies. Bart had put in a very busy week, and a very satisfactory one. He had started in with a system, and had never allowed it to lag. In fact, he improved it daily.

Thanks to his brief, but thorough apprenticeship under his father's direction, he had acquired a knowledge of all the ins and outs of the office work proper.

He had shown great diligence in clearing up the old business. In three days after taking official charge Bart had forwarded to headquarters all the claims covering the fire.

He had also listed the unclaimed packages in the safe, together with those burned up, had followed out Mr. Leslie's direction to collect all not-called-for express matter at little stations in his division, and was now awaiting an order from headquarters as to their final disposition.

The strange "Mr. Baker" had drifted out of his life, temporarily at least.

Bart had purchased the articles the roustabout had required, and that evening Baker came out from his hiding-place marvelously unlike the great-bearded, shock-headed individual Bart had previously known.

A green patch and goggles, a deep brown face-stain, and a pair of thin artistically made "side-burns" comprised a puzzling make-up.

Baker told Bart that he felt himself perfectly disguised, that he could now venture freely down the road a distance where he had business.

"I'll be back, though," he promised. "Perhaps in two weeks. I'm not through with Pleasantville. Oh, no! There's going to be an explosion here some time soon. You've put me on my feet, Stirling, and you won't be sorry when you know what I'm after."

Bart had half planned to hire Baker for what extra work he had to give out. He had to look about for someone else, and Darry Haven and his brother, Bob, alternately came around to the express office before and after school, and helped Bart.

The company allowed for this extra service, but Bart had to take a separate voucher for each task done.

Colonel Harrington had left for a fashionable resort two days after the Fourth, and Bart understood that Mrs. Harrington was preparing to join him there.

Bart's father had been taken home after spending two days in the hospital.

The surgeon there had told him that his case was not at all hopeless, and the old express agent was cheerful and patient under his affliction, and nights Bart made a great showing of the necessity of going over the business of the day, so as to keep his father's mind occupied.

So far Bart's affairs had settled down to what seemed to be a clear and definite basis, and when that afternoon a new platform scale arrived, and he received a letter of instructions from Mr. Leslie concerning the sale of the unclaimed express packages, he felt a certain spice of pleasant anticipation injected into the business routine.

"Why, it will be a regular circus!" said Darry Haven that afternoon, when Bart told him about it. "Last year they advertised the sale at Marion. I was up there at my uncle's. All the farmers came in for miles around, and the way they bid, and the funny things they found in the packages, made it jolly, I tell you!"

When Bart got through with the routine work the next day, he started in to formulate his plans for the sale.

It was to take place in thirty days, and the superintendent had relied on Bart's judgment to make it a success.

Darry Haven came in as Bart was laboring over an advertisement for the four weekly papers of Pleasantville and vicinity.

"Here," he said promptly, "you are of a literary family. Suppose you take charge of this, and get up the matter for a dodger, too."

"Say, Bart," said Darry eagerly, "we can print the dodgers—my brother and I—as good as a regular office. You know we've got a good amateur outfit at home. Father was an editor, and I'll get him to write up a first-class stunner of an advertisement. Can't you throw the job our way?"

"If you make the price right, of course," answered Bart.

"We can afford to underbid them all," declared Darry; and so the matter was settled.

"Oh, by the way," said Darry, as he was about to leave—"Lem Wacker's out of a job again."

"You don't surprise me," remarked Bart, "but how is that?"

"Why, Martin & Company are buying green peppers at seventy cents a bushel. They heard that down at Arlington someone was offering them to the storekeepers at one dollar for two bushels, investigated, detected Dale Wacker peddling the peppers from factory bags, and found that his uncle, Lem, was mixed up in the affair. Anyway, Dale's father had to settle the bill, and they fired Lem."

"Mr. Lem Wacker is bad enough when at work," remarked Bart, "but out of work I fear he is a dangerous man. All right!" he called, hurrying to the door as there was a hail from outside.

Colonel Harrington's buckboard was backed to the platform and its driver was unloading a large trunk.

Bart helped carry it in, dumped it on the scales, went to the desk, got the receipt book, and reading the label on the trunk found that it was directed to Mrs. Harrington at Cedar Springs, the summer resort to which the colonel had already gone.

"Value?" he asked.

"Mrs. Harrington didn't say, and I don't know. If you saw all the finery in that trunk, though, you'd stare. You see, Mrs. Harrington is going to stay three weeks at the Springs, and is sending on her finest and best. I'll bet they amount to a couple of thousand dollars."

Bart filled out a blank receipt, stamping it: "Value asked, and not given."

"It can't go till morning," he said.

"That don't matter. The missus won't be going down to the Springs till Saturday."

"You have just missed the afternoon express," went on Bart.

"Yes, Lem Wacker said I would."

"What has he got to do with it?" asked Bart.

"Why, nothing, I gave him a lift down the road, and he told me that."

The driver departed. Bart stood so long looking ruminatively at the trunk that Darry Haven finally nudged his arm.

"Hi! come out of it," he called. "What's bothering you, Bart?"

"Nothing—I was just thinking."

"About that trunk, evidently, from the way you stare at it."

"Exactly," confessed Bart. "I believe I am getting superstitious about anything connected with the Harringtons or the Wackers. Here, give me a lift."

"All right. Where?"

"Swing it up—I want to get it on top of the safe."

"What!" ejaculated Darry in profound amazement.

"Yes, we don't handle property in the thousands every day in the week."

"But the company is responsible only up to fifty dollars, when they don't pay excess."

"That doesn't satisfy the shipper if there is any loss. I feel we ought to be extra careful until we get a new office with proper safeguards, and that expensive outfit staying here all night worries me. Up—hoist!"

Bart settled the trunk on top of the safe, and on top of that he set the lantern.

When he locked up for the night he lit the lantern, and went over to the freight platform where the night watchman had just come on duty.

Bart knew him well and liked him, and the feeling was reciprocal.

He explained that a valuable trunk had to remain overnight in the express shed, and how he had placed it.

"Just take a casual glance over there on your rounds, will you, Mr. McCarthy?" he continued.

"I certainly will. You set the lantern so it shows things inside, and I'll keep an eye open," acquiesced the watchman.

Bart went home feeling satisfied and relieved at the arrangement he had made.

All the same he did not sleep well that night. About daybreak he woke up with a sudden jump, for he had dreamed that Colonel Harrington had thrown him into a deep pit, and that Lem Wacker was dropping Mrs. Harrington's precious trunk on top of him.

CHAPTER XV

AN EARLY "CALL"

The young express agent was conscious that he shouted outright in his nightmare, for the trunk he was dreaming about as it struck him seemed to explode into a thousand pieces.

The echoes of the explosion appeared to still ring in his ears, as he sat up and pulled himself together. Then he discovered that it was a real sound that had awakened him.

"Only five," he murmured, with a quick glance at the alarm clock on the bureau—"and someone at the front door!"

Rat, tat, tat! it was a sharp, distinct summons.

"Why," continued Bart briskly, jumping out of bed and hurrying on some clothes, "it's Jeff!"

Jeff was "the caller" for the roundhouse. He was a feature in the B. & M. system, and for ten years had pursued his present occupation.

"Something's up," ruminated Bart a little excitedly, as he ran down the stairs and opened the front door. "What is it, Jeff?"

"Wanted," announced the laconic caller.

"By whom?"

"McCarthy, down at the freight house."

"What's wrong?"

"He didn't tell—-just asked me to get you there quick as your feet could carry you."

"Thank you, Jeff, I'll lose no time."

Bart hurried into his clothes. Clear of the house, he ran all the way to the railroad yards.

As he rounded into them from Depot Street, he came in sight of the express office.

McCarthy, the night watchman, was seated on the platform looking down in a rueful way.

He got up as Bart approached, and the latter noticed that he looked haggard, and swayed as though his head was dizzy.

"What is it?" cried out Bart irrepressibly.

"I'm sorry, Stirling," said the watchman, "but—look there!"

Bart could not restrain a sharp cry of concern. The express office door stood open, and the padlock and staples, torn from place, lay on the platform. He rushed into the building. Then his dismay was complete.

"The trunk!" he cried—"it's gone!"

"Yes, it is!" groaned McCarthy, pressing at his heels.

Bart cast a reproachful look at the watchman. The lantern, too, had disappeared. He sank to the bench, overcome. Finally he inquired faintly:

"How did it happen?"

"I only know what happened to me," responded the watchman. "I was drugged."

"When—where—by whom?"

"It's guesswork, that, but the fact stands—I was dosed. You asked me to watch, and I did watch. Up to midnight that lantern on top of the trunk wasn't out of my sight fifteen minutes at a time."

"And then?" questioned Bart.

"I always go over to the crossing switch shanty about twelve o'clock to eat my lunch. The old switchman lends me his night key. I put my lunch in on the bench when I come on duty, and he always leaves the stove full of splinters to warm up the coffee quick. When I let myself in at midnight, the lantern here was right as a beacon—I particularly noticed it."

"How long was it before you came out again?"

"Four hours afterwards—just a little while ago."

"Then you—fell asleep?" said Bart.

"Yes, I did, and no blame to me. I'm no skulker, as you well know. I never did such a thing before in all my ten years of duty here. I was doped."

"How do you know that?" asked Bart.

"I warmed up the coffee and had my lunch," narrated the watchman. "Then I settled down for a ten minutes' comfortable smoke, as I always do. I felt sort of sickish, right away. I had noticed that the coffee tasted queer, but I fancied it might have been burned. Anyhow, half an hour ago I seemed to come out of a stupor, my head fairly splitting, and my stomach burning as though I'd taken poison. I thought of poison, somehow, and more so than ever as I reached over to see if there was any coffee left, for my throat was dry as a piece of pine board. There wasn't, but at the bottom of the pail were two or three little sticky brown dabs. I tasted the stuff. It was opium. I know, for I've used it in sickness. I stumbled out to get the air. The minute I glanced over at the express office I guessed it all out. It's a burglary, right and proper, Stirling, and the fellows who did it knew I was on the watch, got into the switch shanty, fixed the coffee and put me to sleep."

Bart rapidly turned over in his mind all that the watchman had disclosed.

"See here," he said promptly, "how many keys are there to the switch shanty?"

"Only one that I know anything of," responded McCarthy. "There can't be many, or the old switchman wouldn't have to lend me his key."

"Lem Wacker subbed for him once, didn't he?" inquired Bart pointedly.

"Yes, for a day or two—say! you don't think—" began the watchman, with a start of suspicion.

"I'm not thinking anything positive," interrupted Bart—"I am only seeking information. When Wacker subbed for the old switchman, did he have a special key?"

"N—no," answered the watchman hesitatingly, "for I remember Wacker loaned me the old switchman's key the first night. Hold on, though!" cried McCarthy with a spurt of memory, "it comes back to me clear now. The next night he told me to keep the key till the old switchman came back on duty—so he must have had an extra one of his own. They are easily got—it's a common, ordinary lock."

Bart's lips shut close. He went outside, looked keenly around, and jumped down from the platform.

The watchman trailed out after him, watching him in a worried, discouraged way. There was no doubting the word of a trusted employee like McCarthy, and Bart realized that he felt very badly over the matter.

"What is it, Stirling—have you found anything?" asked the watchman eagerly, as Bart, after inspecting the roadway, still more narrowly regarded the edges of the platform boards, running his finger over them in a critical way.

"Yes, I have," announced Bart—"that trunk was taken away from here in a wagon."

"How do you know?"

"Look at those fresh wheel tracks," directed Bart, pointing to the road. "They sided a wagon up to the platform, right here. So close, that a wheel or the body of the wagon scraped along the edges of the boards. The paint was fresh. And it was bright red," added Bart.

"You're a good one to guess that out," muttered the watchman. "Why, say—"

McCarthy gave a prodigious start and put his hand up to his head, as if some idea had occurred to him with tremendous force. "You mentioned Lem Wacker. It's funny, but last week Wacker bought a new wagon."

"Are you sure of that?"

"Yes, it was the same one that his scapegrace nephew, Dale Wacker, was caught peddling the stolen pickles in. I saw Lem painting it fresh out in his shop only two days ago. You know I live just beyond him."

"What color?"

"Red."

"Then Lem Wacker must know something about this burglary!" declared Bart.

CHAPTER XVI

AT FAULT

"I am sorry," again said the night watchman, after a long thoughtful silence on the part of Bart.

"I know you are, Mr. McCarthy," returned Bart, "but nobody blames you. I've got to get back that trunk, though! you are positive about Lem Wacker's wagon being newly painted?"

"Oh, sure."

"And red?"

"Yes, a bright red. Wacker lives near us, as I said. I strolled down the alley day before yesterday. I saw his shed doors open, and Wacker putting on the paint. I remember even joking him about his experience in painting the town the same color once in awhile. He took that as a compliment, Lem did. It seems he traded for the wagon some time ago. He told me he was going to start an express company of his own."

"He seems to have done it—so far as that trunk is concerned!" murmured Bart. "Mr. McCarthy, you and I are friends?"

"Good friends, Stirling."

"And I can talk pretty freely to you?"

"I see your drift—you think Lem Wacker had a hand in this burglary?"

"I certainly do."

"Well, I'll say that I don't think he's beyond it," observed the watchman. "You'll find, though, he only had a hand in it. His way is generally using someone else for a cat's-paw."

"I am going to ask you to do something for me," resumed Bart seriously—"I'm going to get back that trunk—I've got to get it back."

"The company ought to provide you with a safe, decent building."

"That will come in time."

"No one can blame you. They can't expect you to sit up watching all night, nor carrying trunks to bed with you for safe-keeping."

"No, but the head office, while it might stand an accidental fire, will not stand a big loss on top of it. My ability to handle this express proposition successfully is at stake and, besides that, I would rather have almost anybody about my ears than Mrs. Harrington."

"The colonel's wife is a Tartar, all right," bluntly declared the night watchman. "Hello! here's somebody from Harrington's, now."

The same buckboard that had driven up the afternoon previous, came dashing to the platform as McCarthy spoke.

It was in charge of the same driver, who promptly hailed Bart with the words:

"That trunk gone yet?"

"No, not yet," answered Bart.

"Then I'm in time. Mrs. Harrington wanted to put something else in—this box. Forgot it, yesterday," and the speaker fished up an oblong package from the bottom of the wagon.

"It will have to go separate," explained Bart.

"Can't do that—it's a silk dress, and not wrapped for any hard usage. Why, what's happened!" pressed the colonel's man, shrewdly scanning the disturbed countenances of Bart and the watchman. "Door lock smashed, too, and—say! I don't see the trunk!"

He had stepped to the platform and looked inside the express shed.

Bart thought it best to explain, and did so. It made him feel more crestfallen than ever to trace in the way his auditor took it, that he anticipated some pretty lively action when Mrs. Harrington was apprised of her loss.

"You can tell Mrs. Harrington that everything possible is being done to recover the trunk," Bart told the man as he drove off. "Now then, Mr. McCarthy," he continued, turning to his companion, "I am going to ask you to take charge here till I return. I will pay you a full day's wages, even if you have to stay only an hour."

"You'll pay me nothing!" declared the watchman vigorously. "I'll camp right in your service as soon as the seven o'clock whistle blows, and you get on the trail of that missing trunk."

"I intend to," said Bart. "I will get Darry Haven to come down here. He knows the office routine. In the meantime, we had better not say much about the burglary."

"Are you going on a hunt for Lem Wacker?"

"I am."

Bart went first to the Haven home. He found Darry Haven chopping wood, told him of the burglary, and asked him to get down to the express office as soon as he could.

"If you don't come back by nine o'clock, I will arrange to stay all day," promised Darry.

Then Bart went to the house where Lem Wacker lived. It was characteristic of its proprietor—ricketty, disorderly, the yard unkept and grown over with weeds.

Smoke was coming out of the chimney. Someone was evidently astir within, but the shades were down, and Bart stole around to the rear.

The shed doors were open, and the wagon gone and the horse's stall vacant.

Bart went to the back door of the house and knocked, and in a few minutes it was opened by a thin-faced, slatternly-looking woman.

Bart knew who she was, and she apparently knew him, though they had never spoken together before. The woman's face looked interested, and then worried.

"Good morning, Mrs. Wacker," said Bart, courteously lifting his cap. "Could I see Mr. Wacker for a moment?"

"He isn't at home."

"Oh! went away early? I suppose, though, he will be back soon."

"No, he hasn't been home all night," responded the woman in a dreary, listless tone. "You work at the railroad, don't you? Have they sent for Lem? He said he was expecting a job there—we need it bad enough!"

She glanced dejectedly about the wretched kitchen as she spoke, and Bart felt truly sorry for her.

"I have no word of any work," announced Bart, "but I wish to see Mr. Wacker very much on private business." When did he leave home?

"Last night at ten o'clock."

"With his horse and wagon?"

"Why, yes," admitted the woman, with a sudden, wondering glance at Bart. "How did you know that?"

"I noticed the wagon wasn't in the shed."

"Oh, he sold it—and the horse."

"When, Mrs. Wacker?"

"Last night some men came here, two of them, about nine o'clock. They talked a long time in the sitting room, and then Lem went out and hitched up. He came into the kitchen before he went away, and told me he had a chance to sell the rig, and was going to do it, and had to go down to the Sharp Corner to treat the men and close the bargain."

"I see," murmured Bart. "Who were the men, Mrs. Wacker?"

"I don't know. One of them was here with Lem about two weeks ago, but I don't know his name, or where he lives. He don't belong in Pleasantville. Oh, dear!" she concluded, with a sigh of deep depression, "I wish Lem would get back on the road in a steady job, instead of scheming at this thing and that. He'll land us all in the poorhouse yet, for he spends all he gets down at the Corner."

Bart backed down the steps, feeling secretly that Lem Wacker would have a hard time disproving a connection with the burglary.

"Take care of the dog!" warned Mrs. Wacker as she closed the door.

Bart, passing a battered dog-house, found it tenantless, however.

"I wonder if Lem Wacker has sold the dog, too?" he reflected. "Poor Mrs. Wacker! I feel awfully sorry for her."

Bart walked rapidly back the way he had come. It was just a quarter of seven when he reached a half-street extending along and facing the railroad tracks for a single square.

The Sharp Corner was a second-class groggery and boarding house, patronized almost entirely by the poorest and most shiftless class of trackmen.

Its proprietor was one Silas Green, once a switchman, later a prize fighter, always a hard drinker, and latterly so crippled with rheumatism and liquor that he was just able to get about.

Bart went into the place to find its proprietor just opening up for the day. The dead, tainted air of the den made the young express agent almost faint. As it vividly contrasted with the sweet, garden scented atmosphere of home, he wondered how men could make it their haunt, and was sorry that even business had made it necessary for him to enter the place.

"Mr. Green," he said, approaching the bar, "I am looking for Lem Wacker. Can you tell me where I may find him?"

"Eh? oh, young Stirling, isn't it? Wacker? Why, yes, I know where he is."

He came out slowly from the obscurity of the bar, blinking his faded eyes.

Bart knew he would not be unfriendly. His father, one stormy night a few years previous, had picked up Green half frozen to death in a snowdrift, where he had fallen in a drunken stupor.

Every Christmas day since then, Green had regularly sent a jug of liquor to his father, with word by the messenger that it was for "the squarest man in Pleasantville, who had saved his life."

Mr. Stirling had set Bart a practical temperance example by pouring the liquor into the sink, but had not offended Green by declining his well-meant offerings.

Bart remembered this, and felt that he might appeal to Green to some purpose.

"Mr. Wacker is not at home," he explained, "and I wish to find him. I understand he was here last night."

"He was," assented Green. "Came here about ten, and hasn't left the house since."

"Why!" ejaculated Bart—and paused abruptly. "He is here now?"

"Asleep upstairs."

"And he has been here since—he is here now!" questioned Bart incredulously.

"He was, ten minutes ago, when I came down—" asserted Green.

Bart stood dumbfounded. He was at fault—the thought flashed over his mind in an instant.

It would not be so easy as he had fancied to run down the burglars, for if what Silas Green said was true, Lem Wacker could prove a most conclusive *alibi*.

CHAPTER XVII

A FAINT CLEW

"What's the trouble, Stirling?" inquired Silas Green, as Bart stood silently thinking out the problem set before him. "You seem sort of disappointed to find Wacker here. If you didn't think he was here, why did you come inquiring for him?"

"I knew he came here last night," said Bart. "Mrs. Wacker told me so."

"Do you want to see him?"

"No, I think not," answered Bart after a moment's reflection.

"Then is there anything else I can do for you, or tell you? You seem troubled. They say I'm a crabbed, treacherous old fellow. All the same, I would do a good turn for Robert Stirling's son!"

"Thank you," said Bart, feeling easier. "If you will, you might tell me who was with Lem Wacker last night."

"Two men—don't know them from Adam, never saw them before. Lem drove up with them in his rig about ten o'clock. They took the horse and wagon around to the side shed and came in, drank and talked a lot among themselves, and finally started playing cards in the little room yonder."

"By themselves?"

"Yes. Once, when I went in with refreshments, Wacker was in a terrible temper. It seemed he had lost all his money, and he had staked his rig and lost that, too. One of the two men laughed at him, and rallied him, remarking he would have 'his share,' whatever that meant, in a day or two, and then they would meet again and give him his revenge. By the way, I'm off in my story—Wacker did leave here, about eleven o'clock."

"Alone?"

"Yes. He was gone half an hour, came back looking wise and excited, joined his cronies again, and at midnight was helpless. My man and I carried him upstairs to bed."

"What became of the two men?"

"They sat watching the clock till closing time, one o'clock, went out, unhitched the horse, and drove off."

"I wish I knew who they were," murmured Bart.

"I suppose I might worry it out of Wacker, when he gets his head clear," suggested Green.

"I don't believe he would tell you the truth—and he might suspect."

"Suspect what?" demanded Green keenly.

"Never mind, Mr. Green. Can I take a look into the room where they spent the evening?"

"Certainly—go right in."

Bart held his breath, nearly suffocated by the mixed liquor and tobacco taint in the close, disorderly looking apartment.

His eye passed over the stained table, the broken glasses and litter of cigar stubs. Then he came nearer to the table. One corner was covered with chalk marks.

They apparently represented the score of the games the trio had played. There were three columns.

At the head of one was scrawled the name "Wacker," at the second "Buck," at the third "Hank."

Bart wondered if he had better try to interview Lem Wacker. He decided in the negative.

In the first place, Wacker would not be likely to talk with him—if he did, he would be on his guard and prevaricate; and, lastly, as long as he was asleep he was out of mischief, and helpless to interfere with Bart.

The young express agent left the Sharp Corner without saying anything further to Silas Green.

He had his theory, and his plan. His theory was that Lem Wacker, with a perfect knowledge of the express office situation, had "fixed" the night watchman's lunch, and employed two accomplices to do the rest of the work.

When Wacker woke up, he would simply say he had sold his rig to two strangers, and, so far as the actual burglary was concerned, would be able to prove a conclusive *alibi*.

The men who had committed the deed had driven off with the wagon and trunk, and by this time were undoubtedly at a safe distance in hiding.

Bart went home, got his breakfast, told his mother a trunk had got lost and he might have to go down the road to look it up, returned to the express office, found Darry Haven and McCarthy on duty, gave them some routine directions, and left the place.

Darry Haven followed him outside with a rather serious face.

"Bart," he said anxiously, "Mrs. Colonel Harrington drove down here a few minutes ago."

"About the trunk, I suppose."

"Yes, and she was wild over it. Said you had got rid of the trunk to spite her, because she had had some trouble with your mother."

"Nonsense! Anything else?"

"If the trunk don't show up to-day, she says she will have you arrested."

Bart shrugged his shoulders, but he was consciously uneasy.

"What did you tell her, Darry?" he inquired.

"I put on all the official dignity I could assume, but was very polite all the time, informed her that mislaid, delayed and irregular express matter were common occurrences, that the company was responsible for its contracts, counted you one of its most reliable agents, and assured her that very possibly within twenty-four hours she would find her trunk delivered safe and sound at its destination."

"Good for you!" laughed Bart. "Keep an eye on things. I'll show up, or wire, by night."

"Any clew, Bart?"

"I think so."

Bart went straight to the home of Professor Abner Cunningham.

That venerable gentleman—antiquarian, scientist and profound scholar—had a queer little place at the edge of the town where he raised wonderful bees, and grew freak squashes inside glass molds in every grotesque shape imaginable.

He was a friend to all the boys in town, and Bart joined him without ceremony as he found him out on the lawn in his skull cap and dressing gown, studying a hornets' nest with a magnifying glass.

"Ah, young Bartley—or Bartholomew, is it?" smiled the innocent-faced old scientist jovially. "I have a new volume on nomenclature that gives quite an interesting chapter on the Bartholomew subject. It takes you back to the eleventh century, in France—"

"Professor, excuse me," interrupted Bart gracefully, "but something very vital to the twentieth century is calling for urgent attention, and I wanted to ask you a question or two."

"Surely. Glad to tell you anything," assured the professor, happiest always when he was talking, and willing to talk for hours with anyone who would listen to him. "Come into the library."

"I really haven't the time, Professor," said Bart. "Please let me ask if you had charge of getting up that directory of the county that a city firm published?"

"Two years ago? yes," nodded the professor assentingly. "It was quite a pleasant and profitable task. I believe I saw about every resident in the county in preparing that directory."

"I am going to ask you a foolish question, perhaps, Professor," continued Bart, "for an accurate person like you of course took down only correct names, and not nicknames. Here is the gist of it, then. I am looking for two men, and I know only that they live outside of Pleasantville, and call themselves Buck and Hank."

"Well! well! well!" muttered Professor Cunningham in a musing tone. "Hank, proper name Henry; Buck, proper name Buckingham— hold on, I've got it! Come in!" insisted the professor animatedly. "Oh, you haven't time? Buckingham? Sure thing! Wait here, just a minute."

The professor rushed into the house, and in about two minutes came rushing out again.

He had an open book in his hand, and stumbled over flower beds and walks recklessly as he consulted it on the run, spilling out some loose papers it contained, and leaving a white trail behind him.

"You see here the value of keeping notes of everything," he panted, on reaching Bart—"nothing is lost in this world, however small. Here we are: 'County at large.' Now then, in my private notes: 'Allessandro' uncommon name—'look up—probably Greek.' 'Alaric, Altemus, Artemas, Benno, Borl, Bud—derived from Budlongor, Budmeister—Buck'—I've got it: 'Buckingham, last name Tolliver, residence: Millville, occupation none.' Hold on. We've got the clew—now for the town record."

The Professor again flitted away to the house, and darted back again with a new volume in his hand.

"Here you are!" he cried, selecting a printed page. "'Millville, population two hundred and sixty, not on railroad. R.S.T. Tappan, Tevens, Tolliver'—Ah, 'Buckingham Tolliver, Henry Tolliver,' must be brothers, I fancy. That's all I've got on record. Information any use to you?"

"Is it?" cried Bart, in profound admiration of the old bookworm's system. "Professor, you are the wisest man and one of the best men I ever met!"

CHAPTER XVIII

A DUMB FRIEND

At three o'clock that afternoon Bart Stirling sat down to rest at the side of a dusty country road, pretty well tired out, and about ready to return to Pleasantville.

When old Professor Cunningham gave him the names Buck and Hank Tolliver, Bart was positive that the same covered the identity of the two men who had been at the Sharp Corner with Lem Wacker.

Bart had started at once for Millville. His first intention was to get a conveyance at the livery stable, his first impulse to solicit the co-operation of the town police.

While discussing these points mentally, however, a farmer driving west came down the road. He had a good team, said he was passing through Millville, seemed glad to give Bart a lift, and so it was that the young express agent found himself on the solitary lookout there, two hours before noon.

He experienced no difficulty whatever in finding out all about the Tollivers inside of twenty minutes after his arrival.

They were the last members of a shiftless, indolent family who had lived on the edge of Millville for twenty years.

When the father and mother died the family broke up. The two boys, Buck and Hank, kept bachelor's hall at the ricketty old ruin of a house on the river until ejected by its owner for non-payment of rent, and then went to the bad generally.

They patched up an abandoned shack over on the bottoms, the postmaster at Millville told Bart, and lived by fishing, hunting and their depredations on orchards and chicken coops.

In one of their nightly forays about a year previous they were captured and fined heavily. They could not pay the fine and were sent to jail for six months.

About the first of June they were released, came back to Millville, found their old shack burned down, and since then, the postmaster understood, had camped out in the woods, giving the town a wide berth—in fact, only occasionally appearing, to buy a little flour, sugar or coffee, or, mostly, tobacco.

Nobody had seen them for over a week—nobody knew anything of a newly-painted red wagon.

It seemed probable, Bart theorized, that if they had made for hiding in any of their familiar woodland haunts, they had reached the same by driving through Millville before daylight, and when nobody was astir.

Bart finally found a woodcutter who knew where the Tollivers had had their camping place the week previous. He described the spot and Bart was soon there—a secluded gully about two miles from town.

The place showed evidences of having been used as a camp, but not recently, and Bart went on a general blind hunt.

He traversed the woods for miles, both sides of a dried up rivercourse, and inquired at farmhouses and of occasional pedestrians he met.

It was all of no avail. At three o'clock in the afternoon, tired, bramble-torn and a little discouraged, he sat down by the roadside to rest and think. He began to censure himself for taking the independent course he had pursued.

"I should have telegraphed the company the circumstances of the burglary, and put the matter in the hands of the Pleasantville police," he reflected. "If the trunk had belonged to anybody except Mrs. Colonel Harrington, I would have done so at once. Somebody coming!" he interrupted his soliloquy, as he caught a vague movement through the shrubbery where the road curved.

"No—it's only a dog."

The animal came into view going a straight, fast course, its head drooping, a broken rope trailing from its neck.

Bart suddenly sprang to his feet, for, studying the animal more closely, something familiar presented itself and he ran out into the middle of the road.

"Come here—good fellow!" he hailed coaxingly, as the animal approached.

But with a slight growl, and eyeing him suspiciously, it made a detour in the road, passing him.

"Lem Wacker's dog—I am sure of that!" explained Bart, naturally excited. "Come, old fellow—here! here! what is his name? I've got it—Christmas. Come here, Christmas!"

The dog halted suddenly, faced about, and stared at Bart.

Then, when he repeated the name, it sank to its haunches panting, and, head on one side, regarded him inquiringly.

The animal was a big half-breed mastiff and shepherd dog that Lem Wacker had introduced to his railroad friends with great unction, one Christmas day.

He had claimed it to be a gift from a friend just returned from Europe, who had brought over the famous litter of pups of which it was one.

Wacker had estimated its value at five hundred dollars. Next day he cut the price in half. New Year's day, being hard up, he confidentially offered to sell it for five dollars.

After that it went begging for fifty cents and trade, and no takers. Lem kicked the poor animal around as "an ornery, no-good brute," and had to keep it tied up on his own premises all of the time to evade paying for a license tag.

Meeting the dog now, gave a new animation to Bart's thoughts.

The sequence of its appearance, here, ten miles away from home, was easy to pursue. It had broken away from its new owners—Buck and Hank Tolliver—and they were somewhere further up the road.

Christmas was making for home. It was hardly possible that the animal knew Bart, for, although he had seen it several times, he had never spoken to it before. The call of its name, however, had checked the animal, and now as Bart drew a cracker from his pocket and extended it, the dog began to advance slowly and cautiously towards him.

Bart saw the importance of making a friend of the animal. He stood perfectly still, talking in a gentle, persuasive tone.

Christmas came up to him timorously, sniffed all about his feet, and suddenly wagged its tail and put its feet up on him in a friendly manifestation of delight.

Its keen sense of scent had apparently recognized that Bart had been a visitor to the Wacker home that day. It now took the cracker from Bart's hand, then another, and as Bart sat down again stretched itself placidly and contentedly at his side.

"This looks all right," ruminated Bart speculatively. "If I can only get Christmas to go back the way he came, I feel I have found the right trail."

Bart finally arose, and the dog, too. The animal turned its face east, wagged its tail expectantly, and eagerly studied Bart's face and movements.

As he took a step up the road the animal's tail went down, nerveless, and its eyes regarded him beseechingly.

"Come on, old fellow!" hailed Bart encouragingly, patting the dog. It followed him reluctantly. Then he made a rollic of it, jumping the ditch, racing the animal, stopping abruptly, leaping over it, apparently making Christmas forget everything except that it had a friendly companion.

At length Bart induced the dog to go ahead. It led the way with evident reluctance. It would stop and eye Bart with a decidedly serious eye. He urged it forward, and finally it got down to a slow trot, sniffing the road and looking altogether out of harmony with its forced course.

Christmas was about twenty yards ahead of Bart at the end of a two miles' jaunt, when he shied to the extreme edge of the road and drew to his haunches.

Here wagon tracks led into the timber. The road had been used lately, Bart soon discerned.

"Come on, Christmas!" he hailed, branching off into the new obscure roadway.

Bart Stirling's Road to Success

The dog circled him, but could not be induced to leave the main road. Bart made a grab for the trailing rope. The animal eluded him, gave him one reproachful look, turned its nose east, and shot off, headed for home like an arrow.

"I've lost my ally," murmured Bart, "but I think I have got my clew. Christmas does not like this road, which looks as if he left his captors somewhere down its length. I'll try to locate them."

Bart followed the tortuous windings of the narrow road, through brush, over hillocks, down into depressions, and finally into the timber.

He came to a clearing, forcing his way past a border of prickly bushes, the tops of which seemed freshly broken, as though a wagon had recently passed over them.

As he got past them, Bart came to a decisive halt, and stared hard and with a thrill of satisfaction.

Twenty feet away, under a spreading tree, a horse was tethered, and right near it was a red wagon—holding a trunk.

CHAPTER XIX

FOOLING THE ENEMY

Our hero's impulse was to at once spring into the wagon and see if the trunk was still intact.

A natural cautiousness checked him, however, and he was glad of it a minute later as he detected a rustling in the thick undergrowth back of the tree.

A human figure seemed suddenly to drop to the ground, and a little distance to the left of it Bart was sure he saw two sharp human eyes fixed upon him.

He never let on that he suspected for a moment that he was not entirely alone, but, walking over to a tree stump, where, spread out on a newspaper, was the remains of a lunch, he acted delighted at the discovery, picked up a hunk of bread in one hand, a piece of cheese in the other, and, throwing himself on the green sward at full length, proceeded to munch the eatables, with every semblance of satisfaction.

Bart's mind worked quickly. He felt that it was up to him to play a part, and he prepared to do so.

He was morally certain that two persons in fancied hiding were watching his every movement, and they must be Buck and Hank Tolliver.

Bart hoped they had never seen him before; he felt pretty certain that they did not know him at all.

Bart sprang to his feet. He had thrown his cap back on his head in a "sporty," off-handish way, and he tried hard to impersonate a reckless young adventurer taking things as they came, and audacious enough to pick up a handy meal anyhow or anywhere. He paid not the least apparent attention to the wagon or the trunk, although he cast more than one sidelong glance in that direction.

He walked up to the horse, stroked its nose, and said boisterously:

"Wish I had this layout—wouldn't I reach California like a nabob, though!"

Then Bart went back to the stump. He purposely faced the patch of brush where he knew his watchers were lurking.

Ransacking his pockets, with a comical, quizzical grin on his face, he produced a solitary nickel, placed it ostentatiously on the tree stump and remarked:

"Honesty is the best policy—there you are, landlord! and much obliged for the handout."

Then, striking a jaunty dancing step, he started to cross the clearing, whistling a jolly tune.

"Hey!"

Bart half expected the summons. He halted in professed wonderment, looked up, to the right, to the left, in every direction except that from which he was well aware the hail had come.

"Look here, you!"

Bart now turned in the right direction. A man of about thirty had revealed himself from the brush.

He had small, bright eyes, a shrewd, narrow face, and Bart knew from discription who he was—Buck Tolliver.

"Why, hello! somebody here?" exclaimed Bart, feigning surprise and then fright, and he made a movement as if to run for it.

"Don't you bolt," ordered Buck Tolliver, advancing—"come back here, kid."

Bart slowly retraced his steps. Then he manifested new alarm as a second figure stepped out from the brush.

Recalling what the Millville postmaster had told him, the young express agent was quickly aware that this second individual was Buck's brother, Hank.

Buck was the spokesman and leader. He came up near to Bart and looked him over critically.

"What you doing here?" he demanded, with a suspicious frown.

"Nothing," said Bart, with a grin.

"Where do you come from?"

"Me—nowhere!" chuckled Bart, winking deliberately and then, walking over to the horse, he fondled his long ears, with the remark: "If I had a dandy rig like you've got here, I bet I'd go somewheres, though!"

"Where would you go?" inquired Buck Tolliver curiously.

"I'd go to California—that's the place to do something, and make a name, and amount to something."

Bart's off-handed ingenuousness had completely disarmed the men. He pretended to be busy petting the horse, but saw Buck Tolliver slip back to his brother, and a few quick questions and answers passed between them. Then Buck came up to him again.

"See here, kid, are you acquainted around here at all?"

"Did you ever see me around here before?" chaffed Bart audaciously.

"Don't get fresh! This is business."

"Why, yes—I reckon I could find my way from Springfield to Bascober."

Bart had mentioned two points miles remote from the Millville district.

"He'll do," spoke Hank Tolliver for the first time. "Ask him, Buck."

"Do you want to drive that rig a few miles for us for a dollar?" asked Buck Tolliver.

"Me?" cried Bart. "I guess so!"

"Can you obey orders?"

"Try me, boss."

"He'll do, I tell you. What do you want to waste time this way for!" snapped Hank Tolliver irritably.

"Hitch him up," ordered Buck to Bart. "Come on, Hank."

Bart Stirling's Road to Success

Bart chuckled to himself. He did not know what all this might lead to, but it was a famous start.

While he was putting on the horse's harness and hitching him up, the brothers spread a piece of canvas over the wagon box. This they tucked in, and completely covered trunk and canvas with long grass pulled from the edge of a water pit near by.

Bart had the rig in full starting shape by the time they had concluded their labors.

"What's the ticket, Captain?" he inquired of Buck, looking him squarely in the face.

"You seem to know enough not to answer questions about yourself," observed Buck—"try and be as clever if anybody quizzes you about this wagon."

"Why should they?"

"Oh, they may. If they do, you're from—let me see—Blackberry Hill, remember?"

"All right—with a load of garden truck, eh?" propounded Bart ingeniously.

"You hit it correct. What we want you to do is this: Drive down to the main road, and turn west. Keep on straight ahead, and don't turn anywhere. About nine miles west you'll hit Hamilton. Drive right through the town, but as soon as you get out of it take the first branch south from the turnpike, and keep on till you reach an old mill on the river. Wait for us there."

"Why," said Bart, "aren't you going with me?"

"No," answered Buck Tolliver definitely.

"Why not?"

"None of your business," snapped out Hank.

"Oh!"

"You mind yours, strictly, or there will be trouble," warned Buck, and Bart saw from the look in his hard face that he was a dangerous man, once aroused. "You do this job with neatness and dispatch, and it will mean a good deal more than a dollar."

"Crackey!" cried Bart, snapping the whip hilariously—"maybe this is one of those story-book happenings where a fellow strikes fame and fortune!"

"Maybe it is," assented Buck drily.

Bart climbed up to the seat. He started up the horse, the Tollivers following after the wagon till they reached the main road.

"When I get to the mill—" began Bart.

"We'll be there to meet you," announced Buck Tolliver.

"I don't see," growled Hank in an undertone to his brother, "why we would take any risk riding under that grass."

"You leave this affair to me," retorted Buck. "If the kid gets through all right, then we're all right, aren't we?"

"I suppose so."

"And we've got to wait as we agreed—for Wacker."

Bart had just turned into the main road. At the mention of that ominous name, the young express agent brought the whip down upon the horse's flanks with a sharp snap.

CHAPTER XX

BART ON THE ROAD

"Get up!"

The rig that Bart was driving sped along the dusty country road at a good sharp pace.

The young express agent was undergoing the most vivid mental perturbation of his career.

He kept whistling a jolly air, with a sidelong glance observed that his recent companions had turned back towards their camp in the clearing, and then, dropping his assumption of the reckless young adventurer, stared seriously ahead and began to figure out the situation in all its details.

What had come about was quite natural and ordinary: the Tollivers were anxious to get further away from the scene of their recent crime, to a safer and more obscure haunt than the open camp in the woods.

They dared not take the journey in the day time, as they did not wish to be seen by anyone and Bart coming along, they had caught at the idea of sending him on with the wagon and its load.

If Bart got through in safety, they could assume that the hunt for the missing trunk was not very active, or had been started in some other direction.

Bart had comprehended that they could take a short cut to the old mill. He had actually laughed to himself at the ease with which he had obtained possession of the trunk, until they had mentioned that ominous name: Lem Wacker.

"They are going to wait for Wacker!" murmured Bart, as he urged on the horse. "That means that they expect him soon, for they calculate on being at the old mill as soon as I can make it by road. When he does come, and they tell him about me, he's sure to guess the truth. Then it's three to one—get up!"

Bart Stirling's Road to Success

Bart did not allow the horse to lag, but his best pace was a poor shambling trot. All the time Bart thought deeply and practically.

"I have decided," he spoke definitely after a quarter of an hour. "I shall turn to my left the first road I come to. The B. & M. does not touch short of eight miles from here, but somewhere to the southeast is Clyde Station. Once there, I'll risk the rest."

The road was not an easy one. It was not very smooth, and grew more stony and rutty as he proceeded, and there was a sharp climb for the horse as they reached a hilly landscape.

Bart halted finally. A road branched to the left. It did not look very inviting, nor did it seem to be much in use, but as it led away from the main highway, it broke the trail, and without hesitation he turned the horse's head in the direction of Clyde Station.

The country was open here, all rocks, gullies and pits. He was surprised to observe how little distance he had really put between himself and the Tolliver camp as the road wound out along the crest of a hill.

He jumped out to lighten the load and coax up the horse. Then he stood stock-still, straining his eyes across the valley.

"I declare!" said Bart in a tone of profound concern, "I got away just in time, but if that is Lem Wacker, he has appeared on the scene just ten minutes too soon to suit me."

Over at the break in the woods a man had appeared from the direction of Millville. He was waving a hand, and then placing it to his mouth as though hailing someone, probably the Tollivers at the camp.

Then he turned straight around. If Bart could read anything at that distance, he could certainly trace that the man was looking fixedly at the red wagon, and the white horse, and himself.

If it was Lem Wacker—and Bart believed that it was—just one thing was in order: to get that trunk to some town, to some station, to some friendly farmhouse, in hiding anywhere, before the pursuit, sure to follow, was started.

Bart ran on, with a last glance at the lone distant figure. He could not afford to wait to see if the Tollivers joined it. Every minute was precious.

"Where is the horse?" exclaimed Bart.

Dobbin had "got up." While Bart was surveying the landscape, the old animal had plodded on, and was now out of sight.

Bart ran along the road. It turned between two walls of slate. Then came the open again. Here the road descended somewhat. The horse stood at a halt. He had run easily a few rods, one wheel had struck a deep rut, and the wagon had broken down. It lay tilted over on one side, one wheel completely caved in.

Bart was dismayed. He reflected for a moment, and then followed the road ahead for about a hundred feet.

It turned through some slate heaps, lined the side of a deep excavation, and came to an abrupt end where some boards, placed crosswise, barred the sheer descent.

Just such a valley spread out beyond the barrier as on the other edge of the hill whence Bart had seen the man he believed to be Lem Wacker.

Here, however, the landscape was barren in the extreme. There was not a house visible.

Bart was in a dilemma, but he decided how he would act. He first ran back to the spot whence he had last viewed the break in the woods.

A glance stirred him up to prompt and decisive action.

Three men were now in view. They were running at their top bent of speed up the road he had taken.

"Lem Wacker and the Tollivers, sure!" murmured Bart. "They know the wagon is up here somewhere, and they will be here in less than half an hour."

Bart's one idea now was to locate some pit or cranny where he could stow the trunk where it could not be readily found.

This done, he would start on foot in the direction of Clyde Station to get assistance and return before his enemies discovered it.

There were all kinds of holes and heaps around him, but too open and public to his way of thinking. Exploring, he came to the board barrier again, climbed over it, and more critically than before scanned the fifty-foot descent, and what lay at the bottom.

"Why!" said Bart, in some astonishment, "there's a railroad track—"

He leaned over, and scrutinizingly ran his eye along the dull brown stretch of raised rails.

"And a hand car!" shouted the young express agent joyfully.

CHAPTER XXI

A LIMB OF THE LAW

The single track which Bart had discovered lined the bottom of the hill, followed it for a distance, and then running across the valley disappeared in among other hills and the timber.

It was a rickety concern, was unballasted, and looked as if, loosely thrown together, it had never filled its original mission and had been practically abandoned.

"I don't know of any branch of the B. & M. hereabouts," ruminated the young express agent—"certainly none corresponding to this is on the map. It is not in regular use, but that hand car looks as if it was doing service right along."

No one was in sight about the place, yet lying in plain view on the hand car were three or four coats and jumpers and as many dinner pails.

"I have no time to figure it out," breathed Bart quickly. "The first thing to do is to get the trunk down there."

Bart ran back to the wagon. He hurriedly pulled away the grass covering and then the canvas.

The trunk was revealed. He had his first full glance at it since it had been delivered to him at the express office at Pleasantville, the afternoon previous.

"It's all right," he said with satisfaction, after a critical inspection. "There is the paster I slapped over the front. The trunk could not have been opened without tearing that."

He got a good purchase on a handle and landed the trunk in the road. Then he dragged it up to the barrier, removed a board, and, perspiring and breathing hard, held it at the sheer edge of the decline and let it slide.

The hand car was a light-running affair, well-greased, in pretty good order, and he could readily observe was in constant use.

Bart Stirling's Road to Success

Upon it lay the clothing and dinner pails he had noticed from overhead. They evidently belonged to workmen—but where were they?

"I can hardly wait to find out," declared Bart.

He pushed off the clothing and dinner pails and lifted on the trunk.

Then Bart made a depressing discovery—the hind gearing was locked with a chain running from wheel to wheel.

This was unfortunate. Turning a heap of slate, he came suddenly and with delight upon an open tool box.

It was a regular construction case, and full of shovels, crowbars, pickaxes, sledges and drills. Bart selected a crowbar and his efforts to twist and snap the chain resulted in final success. With a thrill of satisfaction he sprang upon the car. The handles moved easily and responsively to the touch.

A grumbling roar caused him to survey the sky, which had been dull and lowering since noon.

"Storm coming," he murmured—"now for action!"

Bart started up the car. It ran as smooth as a bicycle. He was anxious to get away from the face of the hill, not knowing how near the enemy might be.

They were nearer than he fancied, for a sudden shout rang out, then a chorus of them.

A piece of rock, hurled down from the crest of the hill, struck his wrist, nearly numbing it. Glancing up, Bart saw the two Tollivers and Lem Wacker getting ready to descend.

There was a sharp incline and a short curve not ten feet ahead. Bart let the hand car drive at its own impetus.

"Stop!" yelled Buck Tolliver.

He held some object in his hand. Bart crouched by the side of the pumping standard, and the hand car spun out on the tracks crossing the valley, just as the thunder-storm broke forth in all its fury.

Bart Stirling's Road to Success

Bart's back was to the wind, and the wind helped his progress. As the tracks led into the timber, Bart took a last glance backwards, but rain and mist shut out all sight of the hill and his enemies.

He had no idea as to the terminus or connections of the railroad, but never relaxed his efforts as long as clear tracks showed beyond.

Bart must have gone six or seven miles, when he saw ahead some scattered houses, then a church steeple and a water tower, and he caught the echo of a locomotive whistle.

"It's the B. & M., and that is Lisle Station!" he soliloquized with unbounded satisfaction.

Fifteen minutes later, wringing wet with rain and perspiration, Bart drove the hand car up to a bumper just behind a little country depot, and leaped to the ground.

"Hello!" hailed a man inside, the station agent, staring hard at him through an open window.

Bart nodded calmly, consulting his watch and calculating mentally in a rapid way.

"See here," he said briskly, "this is Lisle Station?"

"Sure."

"On the B. & M. Then the afternoon express is due here from the east in twelve minutes."

"You seem to be well-posted."

"I ought to be," answered Bart—"I am the express agent at Pleasantville."

"What!" ejaculated the man incredulously.

"Yes," nodded Bart, smiling. "Won't you help me get this trunk to the platform?"

The station agent came outside and lent a hand as suggested, but he remarked:

"The express doesn't stop here."

"Flag it."

"My orders—"

"Won't interfere, in this case," insisted Bart. "That trunk has got two thousand dollars worth of stuff in it, and was stolen. I recovered it, the thieves are after me, and it has got to go to Cedar Lake on Number 18."

"Well! well! well!" muttered the station agent in a daze, but hastening to place the stop signal.

Bart went inside and unceremoniously approached the office desk. He wrote on a slip of paper, placed it in his pocket, shifted the trunk to the head end of the platform, and stationed himself beside it.

"Is all that you're telling me true?" propounded the bewildered station agent, sidling up to Bart's side.

"Every word of it."

"Where did you get the hand car?"

"I found it. Oh, by the way! I wish you would explain to me about that railroad; what is it, what excuse has it got for existing?"

"Oh, that?" said the station agent "It's the old quarry spur. A company built it five years ago with grand plans for shipping mottled tiling slate all over the country. Their money gave out and the scheme was never put through."

"And the hand car?"

"There's four men who live here who got the privilege of digging out slate for a big plumbers' supply house in the city. They go to the quarry and back on the hand car daily. Did they loan it to you?"

"No," said Bart, "I was in a hurry, and had to borrow it without permission."

"They'll have a fine walk back here in this storm!"

"I was going to suggest," said Bart, taking half a dollar from his pocket, "that you might hire some boy to run the hand car back to the quarry."

"I can do that," answered the station agent.

Bart Stirling's Road to Success

Number 18 came sailing down the rails. As she slowed up, everyone on duty from the fireman to the brakeman was on the lookout for the cause of the unusual stop.

The conductor jumped off and ran up to the station agent, and while the latter was busy explaining the situation Bart hammered on the door of the express car.

"Why it's Stirling!" cried old Ben Travers, the veteran express messenger, sliding back the door.

"You're right, Mr. Travers," assented Bart. "Here's a special and urgent. Get it aboard before the conductor comes up and jumps all over me for stopping the train."

Travers popped down in a lively fashion. They hoisted the trunk together and sent it spinning into the car.

"Cedar Lake, make a sure delivery, Mr. Travers," directed Bart. "Here, put your manifesto on that receipt, will you?" and Bart drew the slip of paper he had written on in the depot from his pocket.

The conductor, a pompous, self-contained old fellow, started towards Bart to haul him over the coals, but Bart wisely walked farther down the platform, the conductor gave the go-ahead signal and shook his fist sternly at Bart, while the latter with a gay, relieved laugh waved him back a cheery, courteous good-by.

Bart told the station agent a very little about the history of the trunk. He left a dollar to pay for the broken hand car lock. He was in high spirits as he caught the east bound train. The whistles were blowing for a quarter of six as he reached Pleasantville and leaped from the engine, where a friendly engineer had given him a free ride, and in three minutes was at the door of the little express office.

Animated voices reached him from the inside. Bart peered beyond the threshold.

McCarthy, the night watchman, sat asleep in a chair in a corner. Darry Haven was at the desk, a spruce, solemn-faced young man beside him.

"I'm here, Darry," announced Bart.

Darry turned with a joyful face. It fell as he glanced beyond his young employer to the empty platform.

"No trunk!" he murmured in a low, disappointed tone.

"Too heavy to carry around, you see!" smiled Bart lightly. "Who is this gentleman? Oh, I see—good afternoon, Mr. Stuart."

"Afternoon," crisply answered the stranger.

He was a young limb of the law, employed since the previous year in the office of Judge Monroe, the principal attorney of Pleasantville.

Stuart was a butt for even the well-meaning boys of the town. He was only nineteen, but he affected the dignity of a sage of sixty, seeming to have the idea that nothing but a severe and forbidding manner could represent the high and lofty calling he had condescended to follow.

"Ah," he observed, turning upon Bart and critically adjusting a single eyeglass, "is this the express agent?"

"That's me," assented Bart bluntly.

"I represent Monroe, Purcell & Abernethy, Attorneys," grandly announced Stuart. "We are employed by Mrs. Harrington to prosecute an inquiry as to a missing trunk."

Darry looked very serious, Bart smiled serenely in the face of his imperturbable visitor.

"What is there to prosecute, Mr. Stuart?" he inquired.

"We have come to demand certified copies of all entries and receipts of this office covering the trunk in question," announced the young sprig of the law.

"Well?" interrogated Bart.

"Your employee—assistant? here, declined to act without your authority."

"Quite right. I give it, though. Darry, make out transcripts of the records. That is all clear and regular."

Bart turned on his heel, ran his eye over the office books, and bored young Mr. Stuart terribly by paying no further attention to him.

The latter stood watching the industrious Darry with owl-like solemnity. Finally the latter handed a duplicate receipt and a copy of the entry to Stuart.

"Will you officially attest to the correctness of these, Mr.—Ah, Mr. Agent?" propounded Stuart.

"Sure," answered Bart with an off-handed alacrity that was distressing to the responsibility burdened personality of the accredited representative of Monroe, Purcell & Abernethy.

He dashed off an O.K. on the two documents, tendered them with exaggerated courtesy to his visitor, who he was well aware knew his name perfectly, and said, with the faintest suggestion of mimicry:

"Ah, Mr.—Representative, would you kindly inform me for what purpose you want these transcripts?"

"They form the basis of a criminal prosecution," announced young Stuart in a tone positively sepulchral.

"So?" murmured the young express agent smoothly. "In that case, let me suggest that you also take a copy of this document to submit to your—superiors."

Bart Stirling drew from his pocket the receipt signed by old Ben Travers on the afternoon express less than two hours previous.

Stuart adjusted his eyeglass and superciliously regarded the document. Then he turned and gasped:

"What—what is this?" he spluttered.

"A receipt for the delivery of the basis of your criminal prosecution," said Bart simply. "Mrs. Colonel Harrington's trunk is safe and sound on its way to its destination."

"Hurrah!" irresistibly shouted Darry Haven.

CHAPTER XXII

BART STIRLING, AUCTIONEER

It was "busy times" at the little express office at Pleasantville.

Bart had made home and lunch in half the noon hour, and entered upon a renewal of his duties with a brisk hail to his subordinates and assistants, Darry and Bob Haven.

On that especial day the services of both had been required. They had arranged to give their full time, and Bart noted that never were there more industrious and enthusiastic colleagues.

There was the sound of active hammering as Bart entered the office, which Darry suspended long enough to remark:

"How's that for the audience?"

The office space proper containing the desk and the safe had been railed off, the express stuff in and out packed conveniently in one corner, and thus three-quarters of the room was given up solely to the requirements of the day.

A dozen rough benches filled in half the space. Its other half, also railed off, held a heap of packages, bundles, boxes, barrels, a mass of heterogeneous plunder, packed up neatly, and convenient for handling.

Beside it was a raised platform, and this in turn held a rough board table on which lay a home-made gavel, and beside this was a high desk holding a blank book and a tin box.

What was "coming off" was the much advertised unclaimed package sale of the express company.

Bart had followed out the instructions received from Mr. Leslie, the superintendent, when he first took charge of the office at Pleasantville, and the sale and its details had been quite an element in his life during the past three weeks.

The various small offices in the division had sent in their uncalled for express matter, and this was now grouped under the present roof.

Bart Stirling's Road to Success

Mr. Haven, an ex-editor, had written up a good "puff" for a local paper, inserted gratis an exciting comment and anticipation in reference to the impending sale, and Darry and Bob had printed fifteen hundred dodgers on their home press, very neat and presentable in appearance, and these had been judiciously distributed for miles around, and posted up in stores and depots.

Bart had heard nothing further from the Harringtons—not even the echo of a "thank you" had reached him. Pleasantville for a day or two had been full of rumors as to the express robbery, but Bart decided to say very little about it, and only his intimate friends knew the actual circumstances.

McCarthy, the night watchman, however, accidentally spread Bart's fame in the right direction. He had a cousin working for the express company in the city to whom he told the story. It got to the ears of the superintendent of the express company.

Bart received a letter from Mr. Leslie the next day, requiring a circumstantial report of the stolen trunk. He answered this and received a prompt reply, directing him thereafter to always report such happenings at once, but his zeal and shrewdness were heartily commended, and a check for twenty-five dollars for extra services was inclosed.

The twenty-five dollars Bart received was the nest egg of a fund being saved up for his father's benefit.

Mr. Stirling could now distinguish night from day, and in a few weeks they intended to take him to an expert oculist in the city for special treatment.

Amid all this encouragement, Bart's life was filled with contentment and earnest endeavor, and he tried to deserve the good fortune that was his lot, and fulfill every duty thoroughly. About a week before the present time he had received a brief letter from his roustabout friend, Baker, dated from a town about fifty miles away, telling him that he had been working on a steady job, but had some business in Pleasantville in a few days, and asked Bart to write him as to the whereabouts of Colonel Harrington.

Bart had replied to this letter, wondering what mystery could possibly connect this homeless vagabond and the great ruling magnate of Pleasantville.

"Now then, my friends," said Bart briskly, as he saw to it that everything was in order for the sale, "the motto for the hour is quick action and cash on delivery!"

About two o'clock there were several arrivals. Half an hour later the place was pretty well filled. There were several village storekeepers, some traveling men from the hotel, and railroad men off duty.

Nearly a dozen country rigs drove up to the platform, and the rural population was well represented.

At three o'clock prompt, as advertised, Bart ascended the little platform and took up the gavel.

Just then he nodded at a newcomer who entered the doorway and quietly took a seat. It was Mr. Baker.

Bart was more pleased than surprised to see him. He had anticipated his arrival the last two days.

Bart tapped the table to call the crowd to order and silence.

Then he looked again at the doorway, and this time with vivid interest.

He saw Lem Wacker shuffle into view, glance keenly around, fix his eye on Baker, and steal into the room and sit down directly behind that mysterious individual.

CHAPTER XXIII

"GOING, GOING, GONE!"

Bart made a first-class auctioneer—everybody said so after the sale was over, and the pleased grins and the good-natured attention of his audience assured the young novice of this as he concluded the introductory speech.

He had prepared a simple, witty preface to actual business, telling many truths of people who had spent a few cents for what had turned out to be worth many dollars, and inviting a good many guesses by hinting what might be in the heap upon which all eyes were fixed intently.

"Number 1129," said Bart, after taking a brief breathing spell.

Bob Haven lifted a box about two feet square to the table.

"Shipped to William Brothers, Ross Junction," announced Bart, reading the tag, "not found. Come, gentlemen! what am I bid for lot 1129?"

"What's in it?" inquired a big farmer sitting near the front.

"You will have to guess that," answered Bart pleasantly. "Ah! some kind of liquid, I should imagine," and he shook the box, its contents echoing out a mellow, gurgling sound.

"Mebbe it's paint, Samantha?" suggested the farmer to his wife. "There'd be two gallons of it—enough to cover the smokehouse. Ten cents."

"The charges are eighty-five," explained Bart—"can't start it any lower."

A blear-eyed, unsteady individual, whom Bart recognized as a member of the Sharp Corner contingent, advanced to the table.

He was thirsty-looking and eager as he poked at the box and tried to peer into it.

"A demijohn!" he muttered, his mouth watering. "Two gallons—probably prime old stuff. Eighty-five cents."

Bart Stirling's Road to Success

"Eighty-five—eighty-five!" repeated Bart.

"Ninety," said the farmer.

"Dollar!" mumbled the thirsty-looking man.

"Do I hear any more?" challenged Bart, gavel suspended, "once, twice, and sold to—cash."

The inebriate paid his money, chuckled and took the box to one side, hugging it like a pet child, reached over and picked up the hatchet from inside the railing, and pried open the corner of the box.

A gleesome roar of merriment interrupted Bart as he called out the second lot.

The inebriate stood disgustedly looking down at the label on the demijohn he had brought to light: "Bubbly Spring Mineral Water."

Lot 943 was a cardboard box. The suggestion of millinery made the farmer's wife a reckless bidder, and the lot brought two dollars.

Another roar went up from the crowd as she eagerly inspected her purchase. It turned out to be a man's silk hat.

She looked spiteful enough to throw it out of the window, but her husband, laughing at her, doffed his worn straw, coolly put on the elaborate headgear, and became thenceforward a target for the quips of the merry idlers about the door.

An oblong crate brought four dollars. Bob Haven got this. He did not inspect his purchase at once, but with glowing eyes whispered to his brother as he pushed it to one side that he knew it was a new bicycle.

Bart hustled the various packages up for sale and disposition with briskness and dispatch, and Darry was more than busy keeping tab on his record book and piling the cash into the tin box.

One fuming, perspiring man, looking too fat to ever get cool, found the prize he had drawn was a moth-eaten fur overcoat.

Peter Grimm, notoriously the stingiest man in Pleasantville, who raised the sourest apples in the town and spent most of his time watching the boys and picking up what fruit rolled outside of the fence, bided his time with watchful ferret eyes until a promising-looking package came along.

It was bid up pretty high, and the crowd urged him to disclose his treasure, but Grimm was not responsive to any mutual human sentiment and sat down with the package in his lap.

He began a secret inspection, however, gradually working off the paper covering at one end, and with snapping eyes worming his fingers inside the parcel.

Suddenly a sharp click echoed out, followed by a frightful yell.

Grimm sprang to his feet, jumping quickly about and swinging one arm wildly through the air, the parcel dangling from it like a bulldog hanging on to a coat tail.

"Murder!" he screamed. "Take it off! take it off!"

Bart had to step down to the rescue. Peter Grimm had drawn a patent mink trap, and was its first victim. He sneaked from the express office nursing his crushed fingers and kicking his unlucky purchase out into the road.

The pile of unclaimed stuff diminished rapidly. The various purchases were productive of all kinds of fun. Tom Partridge, the colored porter at the hotel, got a case of face powder, and an exquisite traveling man for a lace house drew a pair of rubber boots that would fit a giant.

One man disclosed his purchase to be a setting of eggs. They were packed in cotton and intact, though probably a year old.

"Take them out—take them out," yelled the crowd.

Somebody dropped a piece of wood in the box, and there was a pop. The farmer with the plug hat he-hawed at the top of his voice, the miserable owner of the eggs got mad at him, some words ensued, the farmer started after him, the egg owner ran, once outside fired an egg which struck the smooth, shiny tile with a splatter, and the farmer came back into the express office holding his nose, bareheaded, and looking for his rejected straw head-covering.

Some, however, were more fortunate. Bart encouraged and hurried the bidding on a large crate, the contents of which he easily guessed, as did also Tim Hager, the crippled son of a poor widow. Tim got it for two dollars and twenty-five cents, and it turned out to hold a first-class sewing machine.

"Your attention for a few moments, gentlemen," called out Bart as there was a hustle on the part of the audience getting together the mass of stuff they had bought. "All the unclaimed heavy express matter at Pleasantville was burned up in the fire of July third, but some twenty small parcels were in the safe, and those we will now dispose of."

"Money, jewelry, and such, I suppose?" propounded Lawyer Stebbings, who loaned money at a high rate of interest.

"We make no such representations," responded Bart. "I will say this, that no money packages are among the lot. There may be valuable papers, there may be jewelry—in fact, some of the parcels have a given value up to two hundred dollars—but the express company guarantees nothing and you bid at your own risk."

"Good! let's have a sample," demanded Stebbings. "Can I examine? Ah, thanks."

The crowd passed from hand to hand a small well-wrapped package.

"Watch!" hoarsely whispered someone.

"Feels like it!" said a second.

Stebbings bid the lot up to four dollars and got it. There was more fun as he unrolled the numerous wrappings of the package to disclose a small metal disc used in a threshing machine.

One purchaser got a gold pen, another a very pretty stick pin.

Lem Wacker had not engaged in the general commotion. He had retained his place on a bench, looking bored, but for some reason sitting out the session, and Bart wondered why.

Baker took a mild interest in what was going on, smiling appreciatively once in a while when Bart made a witty hit or an unusually good sale.

Finally, however, Wacker put up his forefinger as Bart was bidding off a thin wooden box about four inches square.

"Sender: Novelty Jewelry Company, no address," read Bart, "shipped to James Barclay, Millville—not found. This is a promising-looking package. Gentlemen, what am I bid?"

Lem Wacker seemed to have some spare cash, for he paid two dollars for the box, swaggered off with it, and opening it disclosed a very small and neat pocket alarm clock.

He wound it up, sent out its silvery call once or twice for the edification of the crowd about him, hoping to sell it off to someone, and then, there being no purchaser, with a disappointed grunt slipped it into his pocket.

"Number 529," announced Bart a few minutes later—"the last package, gentlemen!"

The crowd was dispersing, Darry was counting up the heap of bank notes and coin in the cash box, Bob was gloating and wild with delight as uncovering his purchase he brought to light a new bicycle.

The package Bart tendered was thin and flat. Two tough pieces of cardboard held it stiff and straight. It seemed to contain papers of some kind, and so many bidders had bought old deeds, contracts, plans, manuscripts and the like, utterly valueless to them, that the lot hung at twenty-five cents for several minutes.

"Come, come, gentlemen!" urged Bart—"the last may be the best. The charges are sixty-five cents. Sender's name not given. Directed to 'A.A. Adams, Pleasantville'—not found."

"Hoo! S—s—say!"

Bart experienced something of a shock.

The familiar cry of the ex-roustabout, Mr. Baker, rang out sharp and sudden.

Glancing at him, Bart saw that he had arisen to his feet.

His face was bloodless and twitching, his whole frame a-quake. His eyes were snapping wildly. He was like a man who could hardly speak or stand, and fairly on the verge of a fit.

A wavering finger he pointed at the young auctioneer, and gasped out.

"One dollar—two—three!"

CHAPTER XXIV

MR. BAKER'S BID

The attitude, actions and announcement of the mysterious Mr. Baker filled Bart Stirling with profound surprise and wonderment.

The young express agent well knew the erratic temperament of his singular friend, but Baker had been so placid and natural up to the present moment, and this excitable outburst was so vivid and unaccountable, that Bart felt sure that there was some important reason for the same.

All eyes were now fixed on Baker. He seemed to put a dramatic climax to a varied entertainment, and appeared unconscious of everything except the package Bart held in his hand. His eyes were fixed upon this steadfastly—they seemed to burn right into it.

Lem Wacker had also arisen to his feet. Bart noticed him intently studying Baker, sidling up to him and sinking to the bench directly next to him.

There was a suspiciousness in the action that enhanced Bart's interest and curiosity, but he preserved his composure.

"Three dollars, did you say?" he inquired, in an insinuating and soothing, but strictly business tone.

"Yes!" gasped out Baker.

"I am bid—"

"Four."

Bart looked fixedly at Lem Wacker, for it was he who had spoken. Darry Haven dropped the cover of the cash box, and also stared at Wacker. There was something suggestive in the sensation of the moment.

Lem Wacker's face was as bold as brass. He was dressed pretty well and looked prosperous, and there was a mean sneer on his lips as he shamelessly returned the glance of the boy he had wronged, defiantly relying, apparently, on some reserved power he fancied he possessed.

Baker did not even look at the rival bidder. His very soul seemed centered on the package in Bart's hand.

"Five," he uttered with an effort—"six, seven!"

"Eight," said Wacker calmly, striking a cigarette between his lips.

"Ten."

"Twelve."

Baker was silent. A frightful spasm crossed his face. He swayed from side to side. Then, grasping at the bench rails to steady himself, he came up to the platform.

"Stirling!" he panted hoarsely, "I have no more money, but I must—must have that package! Lend me—"

"Whatever you wish," answered Bart promptly.

"Fifteen dollars!" said Baker.

Lem Wacker jumped to his feet, excited. He shot a hand into a pocket, drew it out again holding a pocketbook, ran over its contents, and shouted!

"Sixteen dollars!"

"Twenty!" cried Baker.

"I am offered twenty dollars," said Bart, outwardly cool as a cucumber, inwardly greatly perturbed over the incident in hand, and hastening to close it in favor of a friend. "Twenty dollars once, twenty dollars twice—"

"Stop!" yelled Lem Wacker.

"Do you bid more?" asked Bart.

"I—I do!"

"How much?"

"Double—treble—if I have to!" retorted Wacker. "Only I want you to wait until I can get the cash. I have only sixteen dollars with me—I can get a hundred and sixty in two minutes, I—"

"Terms strictly cash," said Bart simply. "Going, going, at twenty dollars—"

"Hold on! Don't you dare!" raved Wacker, swinging his arms about like a windmill. "I demand that this sale be suspended until I can get further funds."

"Twenty dollars—gone!" sung out Bart in the same business tone, "and sold to—cash."

With a sigh of relief and weakness Baker swayed sideways to a bench, first extending to Darry Haven with a shaking hand a little roll of bills.

"Charge me with the balance," said Bart quickly to his assistant, in a low tone.

"You've no right!" raved Lem Wacker loudly, shaking his fist at Bart, and in a passion of uncontrollable rage. "You'll suffer for this! I protest against this sale—I demand that you do not deliver that package, you young snob! you—"

Lem Wacker was getting abusive. He pranced about like a mad bull.

A heavy hand dropped suddenly on his collar, McCarthy, the watchman, gave him a shove towards the door.

"No talk of that kind allowed here," he remarked grimly. "Get out, or I'll fire you out!"

As Wacker disappeared through the doorway, Bart leaned from the platform.

"Here is your package, Mr. Baker," he said. "What is the trouble—are you ill?"

Baker struggled to his feet. He was in a pitiable state of agitation and nervousness.

"No! no!" he panted, "you keep the package—for a time. Till—till I explain. I've got it! I've got it at last!" he quavered in an exultant tone. "Air—I'm choking! I—I'll be back soon—"

He rushed to the door overcome, like a man on the verge of a fit.

Bart started to follow him. Just then, however, one of the recent bidders came up to ask some question about a purchase which required that Bart consult the record book.

When he had disposed of the matter, Bart hurried to the outside. Baker was nowhere in sight.

CHAPTER XXV

A NIGHT MESSAGE

The crowd had melted away, Bob Haven was totally engrossed with the magnificent prize he had drawn, and Darry was busily engaged in closing up the records of the sale.

Bart was thoroughly mystified at the strange conduct of Baker, and very much disappointed at not finding him, now that he sought the mysterious man.

McCarthy had gone home, and Lem Wacker was not in evidence. Some boys were guarding a pile of stuff that had been purchased and thrown aside. Bart set at work cleaning up the package coverings that littered the place inside and outside.

Things were back to normal when the afternoon express came in. It was nearly two hours late, and closing time.

There was the usual grist of store packages, which Darry attended to, and several special envelopes. These Bart placed in the safe along with the proceeds of the day derived from the sale, barely glancing over the duplicate receipt he had signed for the messenger.

He noticed that two of the specials were for the local bank, and the third for the big pickle factory of Martin & Company, at the edge of the town.

"Both closed up by this time," ruminated Bart. "We can't deliver tonight. Anything very urgent among that stuff, Darry?"

"Nothing," replied his young assistant.

"You can go home, then," directed Bart. "Pretty tired, eh? A big day's work, this."

"Say, Bart," spoke up Darry, as he dallied at the door, "who was the fellow that bought that last package?"

"A friend of mine, Darry," answered Bart seriously. "And I am worried about him. He is the man I told you about who helped me save my father the night of the fire."

Bart Stirling's Road to Success

"He acted very queerly. And Lem Wacker, too," added Darry thoughtfully. "Is something new up, Bart? The way Wacker carried on, he seemed to have some idea in his head."

"He had the idea he could bulldoze me," said Bart bluntly, "and found he couldn't. What bothers me is, why were both of them so anxious to get this package?"

Bart took it out of his pocket as he spoke, nodded good night to Darry, and sat down on a bench, turning the parcel over and over in his hand.

"A.A. Adams," he read from the tag, "a queer name, and no one answering to it here in Pleasantville. I wonder why Baker was so excited when he heard that name? I wonder why Lem Wacker bid it up? Is he aware of the mystery surrounding Baker? Has this package got something to do with it? Wacker looked as though he had struck a prosperous streak, and bragged recklessly about the lot of money he could get. I must find Baker. He was in no condition, mentally or physically, to wander about at random."

The package in question, Bart decided, held papers. It had been given him in trust, and he could not open it without Baker's permission. He replaced it in his pocket and went forth.

Bart visited all of Baker's old familiar haunts in the freight yards, but found no trace of him. Then he called at the Sharp Corner. Its proprietor claimed that Lem Wacker had not been there since noon.

Bart spoke to two of the yards night watchmen. He described Baker, and requested them to speak to him if they ran across him, and to tell him that Bart Stirling was very anxious to see him up at his house.

Affairs at the little express office had settled down to routine when, one morning, Darry Haven dropped into the place.

He found Bart engrossed in reading a letter very carefully. Its envelope lay on the desk. Glancing at it casually, Darry saw that it was from express headquarters.

"Anything wrong?" he inquired, as Bart folded up the letter and placed it in his pocket.

"Not with me, anyway," replied Bart with a smile. "There is something wrong at Cardysville, a hundred miles or so down the main line," he went on.

"And how does that interest you, Bart?"

"Why, it seems I have got to go down there on some business for the Company."

"To-day?"

"The sooner the better, that letter says. It is from the inspector. It is quite flattering to me, for he starts out with complimenting the excellent business system this office has always sustained."

"H'm!" chuckled Darry—"any mention of your valued extra help?"

"No, but that may come along, for you have got to represent me here again to-day, and possibly to-morrow."

"Is that so?" said Darry. "Well, I guess I can arrange."

"You see," explained Bart, "the letter is a sort of confidential one. Reading between the lines, I assume that a certain Peter Pope, now express agent at Cardysville, and evidently recently appointed, is a relative of one of the officials of the company. Anyway, he has been running—or not running—things for a week. The inspector writes that the man has very little to do, for it is a small station, but that very little he appears to do very badly."

"How, Bart?"

"His reports and returns are all mixed up. He doesn't have the least idea of how to run things intelligently. The inspector asks me to go and see him, take some of our blanks, open a set of books for him, and try and install a system that will bring things around clearer."

"Why, Bart," exclaimed Darry, "they have promoted you!"

"I don't see it, Darry."

"That's traveling auditor's work. Besides, a delicate and confidential mission for an official. Wake up! you've struck a higher rung on the ladder, and I'll wager they'll boost you fast."

"Nonsense, Darry, I happen to be handy and accommodating, and they don't want to turn the fellow down on account of his 'pull.' Maybe they think the offer and suggestions of a boy will have a result where a regular official visit would offend Mr. Peter Pope's backer—see?"

All the same, Bart felt very much pleased over this unexpected communication. He blessed his lucky stars that he had such a bright and dependable substitute at hand as Darry Haven.

The latter soon made his school and home arrangements, and Bart left affairs in his hands about ten o'clock, catching the train west after getting a pass for the Cardysville round trip.

It was two o'clock when the train arrived at Bart's destination. He found Cardysville to be a place of about 2,000 inhabitants. Most of the town, however, lay half-a-mile away from the B. < M. Railroad, another line cutting in farther north.

Bart noticed crowds of people and a circus tent in the distance. The express shed was a gloomy little den of a place on a spur track. Near the depot was a small lunch counter. Bart got something to eat, and strolled down the tracks.

As he drew near to the express shed, Bart noticed an old armchair out on its platform.

A very stout man in his shirt sleeves sat in this, smoking a pipe.

He got up and waddled around restlessly. Bart noticed that he approached the door of the express office on tiptoe. He acted scared, for, bending his ear to listen, he retreated precipitately. Then he stood stock-still, staring stupidly at the building.

He gave a nervous start as Bart came up behind him—quite a jump, in fact. Bart, studying his flabby, uneasy face, wondered what was the matter with the man.

"Hello!" jerked out the Cardysville express agent. "Sort of startled me."

"Are you Mr. Pope?" inquired Bart.

"Yes, that's me," assented the other. "Stranger here? looking for me?"

"I am," answered Bart. "My name is Stirling. I work at the express office at Pleasantville."

"Oh, yes, I've heard of you," said Peter Pope. "The express inspector wrote me about you. He said you was a young kid, sort of green in the business, who might drop in on me to get some points on the business."

"Quite so," nodded Bart with a side smile, "catching on," as the phrase goes, and at once falling in with the way the inspector was working matters. "We can't learn too much about the express business, you know, and I thought that by comparing notes with you we might dig out something of mutual benefit."

"You bet!" responded Pope, perking up quite grandly. "The Vice-President of the express company is my cousin. I've got a big pull. Soon as I get the ropes learned, I'm going for a manager's job in the city."

"That will be quite fine," said Bart. "I brought some books and blanks with me, and, if you can spare the time, I would like to have you see how our system strikes you."

"Sure. Come in—no, that is, I'll bring out a chair. I keep only one record. I've got this business simplified down to a lead pencil and a scratch book, see?"

Bart did "see," and knew that the express inspector had "seen," also. He wondered why Pope did not take him into the office. He marveled still more as, watching Pope, he noticed he hesitated at the door of the express shed. Then Pope moved forward as if actually unwilling to enter the place.

Half a minute after he had disappeared within the shed, Pope came rushing out, pale and flustered. He tumbled over the chair he was bringing to Bart, and a book he carried went flying from under his arm into the dirt of the road beyond the platform.

"Why," exclaimed Bart, in some surprise, "what is the matter, Mr. Pope?"

"Matter!" gasped Pope, his eyes rolling, as he backed away from the doorway, "say, that place is haunted!"

"What place?"

"The express room. I've been worried for an hour. It's nigh tuckered me out."

"What has?" inquired Bart

"Groans, hisses, rustlings. I thought a while back that someone was hiding in among the express stuff, and trying to scare me. 'Taint so, though. I went among it, and there's no place for anybody to hide."

"Oh, pshaw!" said Bart reassuringly, "you are only nervous, Mr. Pope. It's some live freight, likely. Can I take a look?"

"Sure—wish you would. I've been posting up on express business, you see, maybe that's the matter. Read about fellows hiding in boxes, and jumping out and murdering the messenger. Read about enemies sending a man exploding bombs, and blowing him to pieces."

"Nonsense, Mr. Pope!" said Bart, "you don't look as if you had an enemy in the world."

"I haven't," declared Peter Pope, "but every business man has his rivals, of course. I've heard that those city chaps have an eye on any fellow that makes a record like I'm making here. They don't want to see him get ahead. They must guess that I'm in line for a big promotion, and that might worry them into playing some tragical trick on me."

Bart wanted to laugh outright. He kept a straight face, and solemnly started to investigate the trouble. He stepped into the express room and took a keen look around, Pope timorously following him.

"There!" panted Pope suddenly, "what did I tell you?"

"That's so," said Bart. "It is sort of mysterious. Someone groaned, sure. What have you here, anyway?"

Bart went over to a heap of express matter, come in just that morning. There were several small crates, a box or two, and a very large trunk. Bart centered his attention on this latter. He stooped down as his quick eye observed a row of holes at one end, just under the hauling strap.

"Quiet, for a minute," he whispered warningly to Pope, who, big-eyed and trembling, resembled a man on the threshold of some most appalling discovery.

Bart's strained hearing shortly caught a rustling sound. It was followed by a kind of choking moan. Unmistakably, he decided, both came from the trunk.

"Is it locked? No," he said, examining the front of the trunk. Then Bart snapped back its two catches. He seized the cover and threw it back.

"Gracious!" gasped Peter Pope.

Bart himself was a trifle startled.

As the trunk cover lifted, a man stepped out.

CHAPTER XXVI

ON THE MIDNIGHT EXPRESS

"Air—and water!" panted the mysterious occupant of the trunk.

Bart looked him over in some wonder. He was a short, wiry man, and arrayed in a close-fitting costume resembling that of the circus athlete on duty.

The man was drenched with perspiration and so nearly exhausted with his suffocating imprisonment, that his voice was rasping and hollow.

He was weak, too. As he stepped over the side of the trunk he staggered feebly. Then, making out an open window and a pail of drinking water on a bench near it, he made a swift dive in that direction.

First the man stuck his head out of the window and drew in great draughts of pure, fresh air.

Then he seized the tin cup near the pail. He dipped up the water and drank cupful after cupful until Bart eyed him in some alarm.

"Ah—h!" breathed the man in a long aspiration of relief and enjoyment, "that's better. Say, ten minutes more and there would have been no Professor Rigoletto."

As he spoke he went back to the trunk. He took out a long gossamer rain coat that had been used as a pillow. This he proceeded to put on.

It came to his feet. He buttoned it up, drew a jaunty crush cap from one of its pockets, and grinned pleasantly into the face of the petrified Peter Pope.

"See here!" blurted out the Cardysville express agent, "this isn't—isn't regular. It isn't schedule, you know."

"I hope not—sincerely," airily retorted the stranger. "Fifty miles on a slow train, three hours waiting in a close trunk. Ah, no. But I've arrived. Ha, ha, that's so!"

He glanced into the trunk. Its bottom seemed covered with some coarse burlap. Professor Rigoletto threw shut the cover.

"Aha!" he said suddenly, bending his ear as a strain of distant circus music floated on the air. "Show on, I'll be late. I'll call later—"

"No, you don't!" interrupted Pope, recovering from his fright, and placing his bulky form in the doorway.

"Don't what, my friend?" mildly asked the Professor.

"Deadhead—beat the express company. You're one trunk—and excess weight."

"I don't dispute it. What, then?"

"Pay," promptly and definitely announced the agent.

"Can't. Haven't a cent. That's why I had to get a friend to ship me this way. But he said he'd wire ahead to my partner with the circus, who would call for me here. I'll go and find him, and settle the bill."

"You don't leave here until those charges are paid. You want to be rapid, too," declared Pope, "or I'll see if the railroad company don't want to collect fare, as well."

"Want to keep me here, eh?" murmured the Professor thoughtfully. "Well, I'm agreeable, only you'll have to feed and bed me. If I'm live stock, I demand live-stock privileges, see?"

The express agent looked worried.

"What am I to do?" he asked, in a quandary, of Bart.

"Oh," smiled Bart, "I guess you had better trust him to find his friend and come back with the money."

"I'll hold the trunk, anyway," observed Pope. "What have you got in it? Some old worthless togs, I suppose."

"Mistake—about a thousand dollars in value," coolly retorted the Professor.

"Yes, you have! I thought so. Some old burlap."

"Careful, my friend!" spoke the deadhead sharply. "There's nothing there that you will care to see."

"Isn't there? I'll investigate, just the same," declared Pope, throwing back the trunk cover and delving in the heap of burlap. "Murder! Help!"

Peter Pope uttered a fearful yell. He backed from the trunk suddenly, A sinuous, hissing form had risen up before his face.

This was an enormous cobra, and, under the circumstances, very frightful to see. The Cardysville express agent made a headlong bolt for the door. He slid clear outside across the platform, and landed in the mud of the road.

"Prt! prt! Caesar, so—so!" spoke Professor Rigoletto in a peculiar, purring tone, approaching the serpent.

He coaxed and forced the big snake back into its warm coverings, and shut down the trunk cover and clasped it. Bart, highly edified at the unique incident, followed him outside.

"I'm the Cingalese snake-charmer," explained Professor Rigoletto. "Sorry, my friend," he observed to the wry-faced Pope, who was busy scraping the mud from his clothing, "but I told you so."

"Ugh!" shuddered the agent. "You get that trunk out of here double-quick, or I'll have you arrested."

"Sure, I will," answered the Professor with alacrity, "and I promise you that I will bring or send you the express charges by the time the show is over."

Professor Rigoletto dragged the trunk to the platform. It was not a heavy burden, now. Bart good-humoredly assisted him in getting it balanced properly on his shoulder. The professor courteously thanked him and asked him to come and see the show free, and marched off quite contented with the result of his daring deadhead experiment.

The Cardysville express agent was greatly worked up over the incident of the hour. It was some time before he could get his mind sufficiently calmed down to discuss business affairs coherently.

Bart, however, handled the man in a pleasant, politic manner, and soon had results working.

He let Peter Pope imagine that he was the originator of every idea that he, Bart himself, suggested. He very deftly introduced the system in vogue at the Pleasantville express office.

In fact, at the end of two hours Bart had accomplished all he had been sent to do. He had got Pope's records into sensible shape, had opened a small set of books for him, and knew that the inspector must be pleased with the results.

Bart had missed the early afternoon train. There was no other running to Pleasantville direct until eleven o'clock that night.

He had planned to put in the time strolling about town, when Professor Rigoletto appeared. He was accompanied by a friend.

The latter ascertained the express charges on the trunk, paid them, and handed both Bart and Pope a free ticket to the evening's entertainment.

Bart took a stroll by himself, got his supper at a neat little restaurant, and met Pope as agreed at the door of the main show tent at seven o'clock.

They were given good seats, and they had the pleasure of seeing Professor Rigoletto and his big snake under more agreeable conditions than those of their first introduction to them.

The show was a very good one, and at half-past ten they left the tent. The Cardysville express agent accompanied Bart to the depot, where the east bound train was due to arrive in thirty minutes.

As they walked up and down the platform, a horse and wagon drove up to the little express shed. Pope went over to it. Bart accompanied him.

The driver of the wagon was a brisk, smart-looking farmery individual. Pope knew him, and nodded to him in a friendly fashion.

"Come after something?" inquired the agent "I don't recall that there is anything here for you."

"No, I want to express these hives," answered the farmer.

He indicated six boxes lying in his wagon, covered with gauze.

"Bother!" said Pope, a little crossly. "That's no midnight job. Why don't you come in the daytime, Mr. Simms? You just caught me here by chance, at this outlandish hour."

"Particular shipment," explained Simms, "and I've got to catch the trains just right. You see, these are special imported Italian bees, Breeders. I reckon every one of those beauties is worth half-a-dollar. They're very delicate in this climate, and call for great care. I want you to instruct the messenger to follow the directions carded on the boxes."

"I can do that," said Pope. "What he will do, is another thing."

"You see," continued the farmer, "if they handle them carefully at Pleasantville, and see that they catch the early express to the city from there, someone will be waiting to take them in charge at the terminus. I'd be awful glad to tip the messenger handsomely to have someone at Pleasantville, where they transfer the hives, open the ventilators for a spell and tip down into the pans some of the honey syrup."

"I will do that for you, sir," spoke up Bart—"I am in charge of the express office at Pleasantville. I am going on this train, and I will be glad to see that your goods are attended to just right, and transferred on time."

"Say, will you?" exclaimed the farmer in a pleased tone. "Now, that's just the ticket! The wrong draught on those bees, or too much bad air, or too little feed, and they die off in dozens. You see, at fifty cents apiece, that means quite a loss on an unlucky shipment."

"It does, indeed, Mr. Simms," responded Bart "I am very much interested in the little workers, and you can rest easy as to their being rightly cared for. I believe I will ride to Pleasantville in the express car, so your bees will be right under my eye till they are put on the city express."

"Thank you, thank you," said the farmer heartily.

As the train whistled in the distance, he came up to Bart and slipped a bank note in his hand.

Bart Stirling's Road to Success

Bart demurred, but it was no use. He found himself two dollars richer for his accommodating proposition.

As the train drew up, Peter Pope rapped at the door of the express car. A sleepy-eyed messenger opened it. The hives were shoved in. Bart made a brief explanation to the messenger, showing his pass. He waved a pleasant adieu to Pope and the farmer as the express car door was closed and locked.

When Bart got home he was more than tired out. But he had done well and in the end got full praise for his work.

A day passed, and Bart failed to find Baker. He hunted everywhere and kept up the search until he knew not where to look further.

Bart went home. He had scarcely reached his bedroom when there was a vigorous summons at the front door.

"I hope it is Baker," murmured Bart, as he slipped on the coat he had just taken off.

"A telegram, Bart," said his mother, at the bottom of the stairs.

She had receipted for it. Bart tore it open wonderingly, glancing first at the signature, and marveling at its unusual length. It was signed by Robert Leslie, superintendent of the express company, at the city end of the line.

This is what it said:

"Special II. 256 by afternoon express, for Martin & Company, Pleasantville, contains fifteen thousand dollars in cash, sender Dunn & Son, Importers. They ask me to make a special delivery, and will defray any extra cost for having it accepted personally by A.B. Martin, and receipted for by him in the presence of witnesses. Delivery to be legal, must be made before twelve, midnight, and this certified to. This is a very important matter for one of the company's largest customers. Be sure to make delivery on time."

Bart read the telegram over twice, taking in its important details, with a serious face.

"Fifteen thousand dollars!" he repeated. "It has saved me some worry that I did not discover the amount before. As to the delivery, that is easy. I've got over two hours yet. I see what it is. Martin & Company probably want to throw up a contract because prices have gone up, the contract must be made binding by payment of fifteen thousand dollars by midnight, or Dunn & Son lose. All right."

His mother noticed that some important business was on her son's mind, and only told Bart to take care of himself.

Bart hurried towards the express office. At a street crossing he paused, to let pass a close carriage that was driven along at a furious rate of speed in the direction from which he had just come.

"Hello!" he forcibly ejaculated, as it flashed by him, the corner street lamp irradiating its interior brightly—"there's queer company for you!"

The remark was warranted. The occupants of the vehicle were Colonel Jeptha Harrington and Lem Wacker.

CHAPTER XXVII

LATE VISITORS

The little express office was dark and lonely-looking when Bart again reached it.

Bart unlocked the office door, shot the inside bolt carefully after him, lighted the lantern, placed it on the desk, and opened the safe.

As he selected the big brown envelope marked "Martin & Company," and bearing the express company's shining green seals, his fingers tingled. The immensity of the sum intrusted to his charge perturbed him a trifle.

Bart relocked the safe, stowed the envelope in an inner pocket, and opened the drawer of a little stand leaning against the safe.

He took out a revolver. Mr. Leslie himself had advised him to always have one handy in the express office. Bart had never touched the weapon before. It had been loaned him by Mr. Haven, and Darry had brought it to the office. Bart slipped it now into a side pocket.

He noticed in detail the entry on the messenger's slip. The prepaid charges on the Martin & Company consignment were seven dollars and seventy-five cents, or five cents for every hundred dollars or fraction of it over the first fifty dollars, which was charged for at regular tariff rates, twenty-five cents.

"It is fifteen thousand dollars, right enough!" mused Bart. "Now, to make sure of the form of receipt."

He filled out a special receipt that acknowledged besides the usual delivery, a verification of the amount of the inclosure, its acceptance as correct, and left a blank for the names of two witnesses.

Bart was now ready to sally forth on his peculiar errand, and had fully decided in his mind the persons he would get to act as his witnesses.

"What is that!" he questioned, suddenly and sharply.

He could hear a springy vehicle bound over the near tracks, and then its wheels cut the loose cindered road leading up to the express office.

It halted. He could catch the quick, labored breathing of two horses, a carriage door creaked! some low voices made a brief hum of conversation, and the vehicle seemed to depart.

Bart stood stock-still, wondering and guessing. Footsteps sounded on the platform. There came a thundering thump as of a heavy cane on the office door.

"Who is there?" demanded Bart.

"Colonel Harrington. I've got to see you."

"Come in," Bart said, unbolting the door.

Colonel Harrington was red of face and fussy of manner. He threw the door shut with his foot, and sank to a bench, breathing heavily.

"Was there something you wanted to say to me, Colonel Harrington?" inquired Bart.

"Yes there was!" snapped out the rich man of Pleasantville. "Anxious to see you! Just drove up to your house. They told me you were here. I once offered you a hundred dollars."

Bart nodded, with a faint smile.

"It wasn't enough," stumbled on the colonel. "I am now going to make it a thousand."

"Why, what for, Colonel Harrington?" demanded Bart in surprise.

"Because you can earn it."

"How?"

"Shall I be blunt and plain?"

"It is always the best way."

"Very well, then," resumed the colonel desperately. "A certain unclaimed express package was sold here to-day, marked A.A. Adams. You've got it."

"How do you know that?"

"Oh, you know it and I want it. Hand it over, and here"—the colonel made a dive for his pocketbook—"here's your thousand dollars."

Bart made a signal of remonstrance with his hand, his face grave and decided.

"Stop right there, Colonel Harrington," he said forcibly. "Are you aware that you are offering a bribe to a bonded representative of the express company?"

"Rot take your express company!" growled the colonel angrily. "I am one of its stock-holders. I could buy the whole concern out, if I wanted to!"

"Until you do, I obey official instructions," announced Bart. "Please do not degrade yourself and embarrass me, Colonel Harrington, by saying anything further on this score. I will not sell my honor, nor swerve a hair's breadth from a line of duty plain and clear. The package you refer to was legally purchased by the highest bidder, I hold it temporarily in trust for him. It is as safe and sacred with me as if it was the property of the First National Bank of Pleasantville."

Colonel Harrington squirmed, got red and pale by turns, gripped his cane fiercely, and then, relaxed with a groan.

"It's my property!" he declared. "I can prove it's my property."

"Then I suggest that you persuade the person who bought it of that fact," said Bart.

"Say!" shot out the colonel eagerly, his eye brightening, "if I bring an order from that same person, will you give up the package?"

Bart hesitated.

"You know where he is, then?" he inquired suspiciously.

"I—I might find him," stammered the military man.

"I do not think I would," said Bart. "Bring him here personally, and I will hand it over to him—in your presence, if he says so."

The colonel groaned again. It was plainly to be seen that he was in an intense inward frenzy.

"Stirling, you've got to give me that package!" he cried, springing to his feet and lifting his cane threateningly.

"Have I?" said Bart, facing him watchingly.

"Be careful, Colonel Harrington! you are pretty near committing a criminal offense."

"You're in the plot—you know all about it! Give up that package, or—or—"

"Colonel Harrington," said Bart calmly, but every word ringing out as clear as the tone of a bell, "I am no ruffian, and I hate violence, but if you lift that cane to me again—I'll shoot."

Bart showed the gleaming top of the weapon in his pocket, backing to the door.

Just then the door behind him was forcibly thrust open, its edge hitting him violently. Then someone pounced upon him.

The attack was sudden and effective. A piece of rope was looped deftly about Bart's arms, holding him helpless, secured behind, and as he was pushed roughly against the desk. Lem Wacker's evil face leered down upon him.

"Don't you holler!" ordered Lem.

As he spoke, he leaned over the railing. The waste box held a mass of cotton that had packed some of the parcels disposed of at the sale that afternoon. Lem grabbed up a handful, and forcibly stuffed it into Bart's mouth.

"Wacker! Wacker!" gasped Colonel Harrington in affright, "don't—don't hurt him. This is dreadful—"

"Shut up!" ordered Lem Wacker recklessly, "you want something and don't know how to get it. I do—and will."

He snatched at Bart's tightly-buttoned coat and tore it loose, groped inside and drew out a package.

"I've got it," he announced. "No!—he ripped off the end of the parcel—here's a haul."

Bart writhed, choked on the loose strangling filaments of cotton, but could not utter a word.

"Give me that package!" cried the colonel. "Stop! where are you going?"

Lem Wacker had bolted. The colonel stared in marveling astonishment as his cohort sprang through the open doorway. Bart had managed to wad the cotton in his mouth into a compact wet mass, enabling him to speak.

"Colonel Harrington!" he cried, "that man has not got the package you were after. He has instead stolen a money envelope for Martin & Company containing fifteen thousand dollars in currency, and is making off with it. Cut this rope instantly that I may pursue him, or I give you my word that, as a partner in his crime, rich as you are, and influential as you are, you shall go to the State penitentiary."

CHAPTER XXVIII

THIRTY SECONDS OF TWELVE

It was an exciting moment. Bart was intently worked up, but he kept his head level. Everything hung on the action of the next two minutes.

Whatever price the rich Colonel Harrington was paying Lem Wacker for his coöperation, it was not enough to blind that individual to a realization of the fact that accident had placed in Wacker's grasp the great haul of his life, and he was making off with this fortune, leaving the colonel in the lurch.

The latter stood shaking like an aspen, his face the color of chalk. Apparently he took in and believed every word that Bart had spoken.

"I'm in a fix—a terrible fix!" he groaned. "This is dreadful—dreadful!"

"Mend it, then!" cried Bart. "Quick! if you have one spark of sense or manhood in you. There's a knife—cut this rope."

With quivering fingers Colonel Harrington took up from the desk the office knife used for cutting string. It was keen-bladed as a razor. Unsteady and bungling as was his stroke, he severed the rope partly, and Bart burst his bonds free.

"Stay here," called out the young express agent sharply. "I hold you responsible for this office till I return!"

He dashed outside like a rocket, scanned the whole roadway expanse, and darted for the freight yards with the speed of the wind.

The electric arc lights were sparsely scattered, but there was sufficient illumination for him to make out a fugitive figure just crossing the broad roadway towards the freight tracks.

It was Lem Wacker. A train of empty box freights blocked his way. He stooped, made a diving scurry under one of them, and was lost to view.

Bart ran as he had never run before. The train cleared the tracks as he reached the spot where Wacker had disappeared.

At that moment above the jangling, clumping activity of the yards there arose on the night air one frightful, piercing shriek.

Bart halted with a nameless shock, for the utterance was distinctly human and curdling. He glanced after the receding train, fancying that Wacker might have got caught under the cars and was being dragged along with them.

That roadbed was clear, however. Two hundred feet to the right was a second train. Its forward section was moving off, having just thrown some cars against others stationary on a siding.

Bart ran towards these. Wacker could not have so suddenly disappeared in any other direction. He crossed between bumpers, and glanced eagerly all around. There was no hiding-place nearer than the repair shops, and they were five hundred feet distant.

Wacker could not possibly have reached their precincts in the limited space of time afforded since Bart had last lost sight of him.

"He is hiding in some of those cars," decided Bart, "or he has swung onto the bumpers of the section pulling out—hark!"

Bart pricked up his ears. A strange sound floated on the air—a low, even, musical tinkle.

Its source could not be far distant. Bart ran along the side of the stationary freights.

"It is Wacker, sure," he breathed, "for that is the same sound made by the little alarm clock he bought at the sale this afternoon."

The last vibrating tintinnabulations of the clock died away as Bart discovered his enemy.

Lem Wacker's burly figure and white face were discernible against the direct flare of an arc light. He seemed a part of the bumpers of two cars. Bart flared a match once, and uttered the single word:

"Caught."

Lem Wacker was clinging to the upright brake rod, and swaying there. His face was bloodless and he was writhing with pain. One foot was clamped tight, a crushed, jellied mass between two bumpers.

It seemed that his foot must have slipped just as the forward freights were switched down. This had caused that frenzied yell. Perhaps the thought of the money had impelled him not to repeat it, but the little alarm clock which he carried in his pocket had betrayed him.

Bart took in the situation at a glance. He was shocked and unnerved, but he stepped close to the writhing culprit.

"Lem Wacker," he said, "where is that money envelope?"

"In my pocket," groaned Wacker. "I've got it this time—crippled for life!"

The young express agent did not have to search for the stolen money package. It protruded from Wacker's side pocket. As he glanced it over, he saw that it was practically intact. Wacker had torn open only one corner, sufficient to observe its contents. Bart placed the envelope in his own pocket.

"I'm fainting!" declared Wacker.

Bart crossed under the bumpers to the other side of the freights. He swept the scene with a searching glance, finally detected the shifting glow of a night watchman's lantern, and ran over to its source.

He knew the watchman, and asked the man to accompany him, explaining as they went along that Lem Wacker had got caught between two freights, was held a prisoner in the bumpers with his foot crushed, and pointed the sufferer out as they neared the freights.

Wacker by this time had sunk flat on the bumpers, his limbs twisted up under him, but he managed to hold on to the brake rod. He only moaned and writhed when the horrified watchman spoke to him.

"I'll have to get help," said the latter. "They will have to switch off the front freights to get him loose."

The watchman took out his whistle and blew a kind of a call on the telegraphic system. Two minutes later Bart saw McCarthy hurriedly rounding a corner of the freight depot, and advanced towards him.

The young express agent briefly and confidentially imparted to his old friend the fact that Lem Wacker had tried to steal some money from the express office, and had got his deserts at last.

"Get him clear of the bumpers," said Bart, "carry him to the express office, call for a surgeon, and don't let him be taken away from there till I show up."

"What's moving, Stirling?" inquired McCarthy.

"Something very important. Wacker seems to be punished enough already, and I do not know that I want him placed under arrest, but he knows something he must tell me before he gets out of my reach."

"Then you had better wait."

"I can't do that," said Bart. "I have a special to deliver, on personal orders from Mr. Leslie, the express superintendent."

Bart consulted his watch. It was five minutes of eleven.

"Only a little over an hour," he reflected. "I want to hustle!"

He saw to it that the recovered package was safely stowed in an inner pocket, and started by the shortest cut he knew from the yards.

Bart did not even pause at the express office, where he had left Colonel Harrington. He ran all the way half across the silent, sleeping town, and never halted until he reached the Haven homestead.

He did not go to the front door, but, well acquainted with the disposition of the household, paused under a rear window, picked up a handful of gravel, threw it against the upper panes, and gave three low but distinct whistling trills.

He could hear a prompt rustling. In less than forty seconds Darry Haven stuck his head out of the window.

"Hello!" he hailed, rubbing his eyes.

"Come down, quick," directed Bart. "Bring Bob, too."

"What's the lark, Bart?"

Bart Stirling's Road to Success

"No lark at all," answered Bart—"strictly business. Don't take a minute. No need disturbing the folks. You can be back inside of an hour."

Bob, hatless and without a collar, came sliding down the lightning rod two minutes later. Darry landed on the ground almost simultaneously, simply letting himself drop from the window sill.

"Two dollars apiece for half an hour's work," said Bart, and then told his companions the details of the special mission in which he required their services.

"Ginger! but you're nerve and action," commented the admiring Bob.

"And good to your friends," put in Darry.

They passed the pickle factory. It stood on the edge of the town, and the residence of the senior partner of Martin & Company, whose name had been mentioned in the telegram, was nearly half a mile further away.

"Eleven thirty-five," announced Bart, a trifle anxiously. "It does not give us much time. I hope there's no slip anywhere."

At just fifteen minutes of midnight the strange trio passed up the graveled walk leading to the Martin mansion. The front door had a ponderous old-fashioned knocker, and Bart plied it without ceremony.

He began to grow nervous as three minutes passed by, and not the least attention was paid to his summons.

Suddenly an upper window was thrust up, and a man's head came into view.

"Who's there?" demanded a gruff, impatient voice.

"Is this Mr. Martin, Mr. A.B. Martin?" inquired Bart.

"Yes, it is—what do you want?"

"I have an express package for you," explained Bart.

"Oh, you have?" snapped Mr. Martin. "What the mischief do you mean waking a man up at midnight on a thing like that! Deliver it at the factory in the morning."

The speaker, muttering direfully under his breath, was about to slam down the window.

"Wait one moment, Mr. Martin," called up Bart sharply. "This is a special delivery, and a very important matter. I tender you this package in the presence of these witnesses, and it is a legal delivery. If you decline to come down and take it, and I leave it on your doorstep at the call of the first tramp who happens to come along, I have done my duty, and the loss is yours—a matter of fifteen thousand dollars."

"What! what!" shouted Martin.

"That is the amount."

"From—Dunn & Son?"

"I guess that's right," said Bart. "Will you come down and take it?"

Martin did not reply. He disappeared from the window, but left it open. Bart heard him muttering to himself.

"Supposing he doesn't come down?" questioned Bob, in a whisper.

"I think he will," said Bart. "Eleven forty-eight. Mr. Martin," he called out loudly, "I can't wait here all night."

"Shut up!" retorted an angry voice—"I'm hurrying all I can."

"He isn't!" spoke Darry, in a low tone to Bart. "He's on to the business, and playing for time."

"And he's beat us!" breathed Bob—"hear there! twelve o'clock. Your delivery is no good, Bart! It's just struck a new day!"

"S—sh!" warned Bart, as a clock inside the house rang out twelve silvery strokes. "The clock is wrong. We've got five minutes and a half yet."

In about two minutes a light flashed in the hall, the front door was unlocked, and Martin appeared, half-dressed. Bart relievedly put up his watch. It was just three minutes of twelve.

He instantly placed the express envelope in Martin's hands, slipping into the vestibule.

"Mr. Martin," he said, "it is necessary for you to verify the contents of this package. An accident happened to it, as you see."

Martin tore the envelope clear open, and glanced over fifteen bills of one thousand dollar denomination each.

"All right," he said gruffly.

"Will you sign this receipt?" asked Bart politely, tendering the slip of paper he had prepared at the office for this especial occasion. "Thank you," he added, as the pickle man scrawled a penciled signature at the bottom of the paper.

"I take this money," said Mr. Martin, looking up with a peculiar expression on his face, "because it is delivered by you, but I shall return it to Dunn & Son to-morrow."

"That is your business, Mr. Martin," said Bart politely.

"It is, and—something more! I call on you and your witnesses to notice that the fifteen thousand dollars was not delivered to me until six minutes after twelve, too late to make the tender legal, which makes the contract null and void."

Mr. Martin, with a triumphant sweep of his hand, pointed to a big clock at the end of the long hall.

"I beg your pardon," said Bart, holding up his watch, "but I keep official time, and it is exactly thirty seconds to midnight. Listen!"

And thirty seconds later, from the Pleasantville court house tower, the town bell rang out twelve musical strokes.

CHAPTER XXIX

BROUGHT TO TIME

"I'll go!" said Colonel Jeptha Harrington, magnate of Pleasantville.

"All right," said Bart Stirling, express company agent.

It was three o'clock in the morning, and the scene was the little express office where so many unusual and exciting happenings had transpired within twenty-four hours.

The colonel's announcement was given in the tone of a man facing a hard proposition and forced to accept it—or something worse.

Bart's reply was calm and off-handed. During a two hours' siege with the military man he had never lost his temper or his wits, and had come off the victor.

When Bart had concluded his very creditable piece of business with Mr. Martin of the pickle factory, he had sent Darry and Bob Haven back to bed, and had forthwith returned to the express office.

Colonel Harrington, scared-looking and sullen, was still there. He seemed to have met his match in the young express agent, and dared not defy him.

Bart found McCarthy, the night watchman, on guard outside, who told him that they had got Lem Wacker clear of the bumpers, had carried him into the express office, made up a rude litter, and had sent for a surgeon.

The latter had just concluded his labors as Bart entered. Lem Wacker lay with his foot bandaged up, conscious, and in no intense pain, for the surgeon had given him some deadening medicine.

"He belongs at the hospital," the surgeon advised Bart. "That foot will have to come off."

"As bad as that!" murmured Bart.

"Yes. I will telephone for the ambulance when I leave here."

"Very well," acquiesced Bart. "Can I speak with the patient?"

"If he will speak with you. He's an ugly, ungrateful mortal!"

Bart went over to the side of the prostrate man.

"Mr. Wacker," he said, "I do not wish to trouble you in your present condition, but something has got to be understood before you leave this place. You go to the hospital as a prisoner or as a patient, just as you elect."

"Pile it on! pile it on!" growled Wacker. "You've got the upper hand, and you'll squeeze me, I suppose. All the same, those who stand back of me will take care of me or I'll explode a bomb that will shatter Pleasantville to pieces!"

Colonel Harrington shuddered at this palpable allusion to himself.

"And I'm going to sue the railroad company for my smashed foot. What do you want?"

"This, Mr. Wacker," pursued Bart quietly, "you have to-night committed a crime that means State's prison for ten years if I make the complaint."

"I'll have a partner in it, all the same!" remarked Wacker grimly.

The colonel groaned.

"You were after a package that belongs to a friend of mine," continued Bart. "I want to know why, and I want to know what you have done with that person."

"Don't you torture me!" cried Wacker irritably—"don't you let him," he blared out to the quacking magnate. "I won't say a word. Let Harrington do as he pleases. He's the king bee! Only, just this, Harrington, you take care of me or I'll blow the whole business."

"Yes, yes," stammered the colonel in a mean, servile way, approaching the litter, "leave it all to me, Wacker. Don't raise a row, Stirling," he pleaded piteously, "don't have him arrested, I'll foot the bill, I'll square everything. This matter must be hushed—yes, yes, hushed up!" hoarsely groaned the military man. "Oh, its dreadful, dreadful!"

Bart felt that he had matters in strong control, spoke a word to McCarthy and, when the ambulance came, allowed them to take Lem Wacker to the hospital.

Then he and Colonel Harrington were alone. The latter was in a pitiable condition of fear and humiliation.

"See here, Stirling," he said finally, "I'll confess the truth. I've done wrong. There's a paper in that package that would mean disgrace for me if it was made public. I'll own to that, but it's over a dead and buried business, and it can do no good to make it public property now. I warn you if it is, I will shoot myself through the head."

Bart doubted if the colonel had the courage to carry out his threat, but he temporized with the great man, got him to make enough admissions to somewhat clear the situation, and the long discussion ended with the announcement by Colonel Harrington that he "would go."

In other words, he confessed that Baker, Bart's friend and the highest bidder for the mysterious express package, was a prisoner in his barn.

In some way Lem Wacker had become aware of Baker's secret, whatever that was, and had helped the colonel in his efforts to suppress Baker and secure possession of the package.

Bart was shocked at this exhibition of cold-blooded villainy on the part of a representative member of the community, although he had never had much use for the pompous, domineering old tyrant, who now led the way through the silent Streets of Pleasantville as meek as a lamb.

He took Bart through the beautiful grounds of his sumptuous home, and to a windowless padlocked room in the loft of the stable.

Poor Baker, his hands secured with stout pieces of wire, arose from a stool with a gleam of hope on his pallid face as Bart followed the colonel into the room.

"See here, Baker—which isn't your name—but it will do—" said the colonel at once, "things have turned your way. Your friend here, young Stirling, has got the whip-hand—I am cornered, and admit it.

Bart Stirling's Road to Success

I want to make a proposition to you, Stirling needn't hear it. When you have decided, we will call him into the room again and he will see that you get your rights. Is that satisfactory?"

"What shall I do?" asked Baker of Bart.

"Hear what Colonel Harrington has to say. If it suits you, settle up this matter as you think right. I am here to see that he does as he promises."

Bart stepped out of the room. There was a continuous hum of conversation for nearly half an hour. Then the colonel opened the door.

"I'm to go into the house to write out something Baker wants," he explained. "Then I'll come back."

"Very well," nodded Bart.

He tried to engage Baker in conversation, but the latter, his hands free now, paced the room nervously, acting like some caged animal.

"I'm afraid of him!" he declared. "I don't know that I am doing what is best. He's a bad man. He begs me to spare him for the sake of his family."

"Is this a matter where settlement will do any injustice to others?" asked Bart.

"None, now—it is past that."

"Then follow the dictates of your own judgment, Mr. Baker," directed Bart, "being sure that you are acting with a clear conscience."

Colonel Harrington, when he returned, brought two documents. Baker looked them over.

"Are they satisfactory?" inquired the colonel anxiously.

"Yes," answered Baker.

"Now understand, there is to be no gossip about this affair?" insisted the magnate.

"I shan't talk," said Baker.

"And I am to have that express package?"

"Give it to him, Stirling."

Bart took the mysterious unclaimed package from his pocket. Colonel Harrington seized it with a satisfied cry.

"You have wronged myself and others deeply, Colonel Harrington," said Baker in a grave, reproachful tone, "but you have made some amends. I forgive you, and I hope you will be a better man."

CHAPTER XXX

"STILL HIGHER!"

Bart Stirling was a proud and happy boy as he stood at the door of the express office looking down the tracks of the B. & M.

A new spur was being constructed, and it divided to semi-inclose a substantial foundation which was the start of the new and commodious express office. The blue sky, smiling down on the busy scene, was no more serene than the prospect which the future seemed to offer for the successful young express agent.

With his last reckless crime Lem Wacker had ceased to be a disturbing element at Pleasantville. After two months' confinement he had limped out of the hospital, out of town, and out of Bart Stirling's life.

Colonel Jeptha Harrington himself had left town with the beginning of winter. It was said he intended to make an extended trip in Europe.

With his departure, a new Mr. Baker seemed to spring into existence. Divested of his disguise, no longer a fear-filled roustabout fugitive, Bart's strange friend had found a steady, lucrative position at the hotel, and Bart felt that he had certainly been the means of doing some real good in the world every time he looked at the happy, contented face of his protégé.

Concerning all the details of Baker's past, Bart never knew the entire truth.

Baker felt, however, that it was due to his champion that he explain in the main the mystery of his connection with Colonel Harrington, and he told a strange story.

It seemed that the purse-proud colonel had a poor brother living in another State.

This brother owned a farm on which there lived with him a man named Adams, a widower, and his little daughter, Dorothy.

Adams was a close friend of Samuel Harrington, and out of his earnings saved the place from being taken on a mortgage.

Samuel Harrington always told Adams that he had made a will, and that in case of his sudden death the farm would go to him. He gave Adams a letter certifying to his having a claim of over three thousand dollars against the property, which he told Adams to show to his rich brother when he died, asserting that, although Colonel Harrington had shamefully neglected him, he would never dishonorably repudiate a claim of that kind.

When Samuel Harrington died, his brother appeared, took possession of the farm as only heir, and cruelly drove Mr. Adams and his child from the place.

He tore up the written statement Adams gave him, ridiculed his claims, and, no will being found, sold the place for a song and left Adams an invalid pauper.

Adams had done Baker, or, as his real name was, Albert Baker Mills, a great service once.

Baker, or Mills, supported Adams and his child for a year. Adams spent all his time bemoaning his fate, and haunted the old farm in a search of the will of Samuel Harrington.

One day he did not appear, nor the following. Early on the morning of the third day he staggered into the house, weak and fainting. He was taken down with a fever, was delirious for a week, and at the end of that time died.

Just before his death he tried to tell something about the will. Baker made out that he had found it, that it was at Pleasantville, nothing more.

After his friend's death, Baker wrote a letter to Colonel Harrington. He accused him of his dishonorable conduct, and threatened to publicly expose him if he did not provide in some way for the little orphan, Dorothy, for whom he had found a home with a poor relative.

A week later Colonel Harrington sought out Baker, told him he had trumped up a charge against him that would land him in jail, which

Baker later discovered was the truth, and gave him twenty-four hours to leave the country.

From that time the poor fellow was a fugitive, venturing to appear only in disguise at Pleasantville. Adams, it seemed, had found the will and had sent it to Pleasantville addressed to himself, not daring to face the colonel with the important document in his possession, but never living to carry out his plan.

In the settlement with Colonel Harrington, Baker had received a letter exculpating him totally from the trumped up charge, and a check for five thousand dollars, which money was now held in trust by a bank to provide for little Dorothy's future.

Bart felt much gratified over the way all these tangled strands in the warp and woof of his young life had been straightened out, but he experienced a final blessing that filled him with unutterable joy and gratefulness.

A week previous his father had returned from a month's treatment by a city expert oculist.

Robert Stirling came back to Pleasantville a well man.

That was a joyful night at the little Stirling home, when Mr. Stirling once again looked with restored sight upon the faces of the many friends who respected and loved him.

Mr. Stirling, while in the city, had been an invited guest at the home of Mr. Leslie, and the express superintendent had learned a good deal more about his devoted son than he had ever known before.

"Come out of it!" hailed a jolly voice, and Bart was disturbed in his pleasant reverie by the appearance of Darry and Bob Haven.

"It's settled!" cried the latter ecstatically?—"we're going into the regular business at last."

"I don't quite catch on," returned Bart.

"The printing and publishing business," put in Darry. "We have got the money together for a nice little plant, and father and mother are willing that we shall go ahead. Some day you'll see us running a regular newspaper."

"Well, I wish you good luck—you certainly deserve it," answered the young express agent, warmly.

"There is only one drawback," resumed Bob. "We'll have to give up helping you."

"Don't let that bother you. I'll find somebody else. Say, it will be fine to start a regular newspaper," went on Bart. "I guess you'd wake some of the old-timers up—they are so moss-eaten. This town needs a bright, up-to-date sheet."

"We are going to push the printing and publishing business all we can," answered Darry, earnestly. How he and his brother carried out their project I shall relate in another story, to be called, "Working Hard to Win." It was no light undertaking, but the boys entered into it with a vigor that was bound to command success.

"You see, father can help us a good deal," said Bob. "He used to be an editor, you know. And more than that, mother can make us whatever pictures we may need."

"Oh, you'll be right in it, I know," laughed Bart. "When you start your newspaper put me down as the first subscriber. Your subscription money is ready whenever you want it."

At that moment a messenger appeared.

"Letter for you," said he to the young express agent, and hurried about his business.

"From the express people," murmured Bart, tearing open the letter.

As he perused it, such a quick, bright glow flashed into his face and eyes, that the watchful Darry at once surmised that Bart had received a communication out of the ordinary.

"Good news, Bart?" he inquired.

"Read it," said Bart simply, and quick-witted Darry saw that he was almost too overcome to speak further.

The letter was from Mr. Leslie the superintendent, and contained two paragraphs.

The first stated that from the fifteenth of the coming month Mr. Robert Stirling would resume his position as express agent at

Pleasantville, thenceforward made a "Class B" station, at a salary of seventy dollars a month.

The second paragraph requested Mr. Bart Stirling to report at headquarters for assignment to duty at a city office as assistant manager.

Darry Haven reached out and caught the hand of his loyal friend in a warm, glad clasp.

"Capital!" he cried enthusiastically—"in line with your motto, Bart Stirling—higher still!"

THE END

Copyright © 2023 Esprios Digital Publishing. All Rights Reserved.